Bad Day in Dirtwood

When Luke McCoy killed his first man, the townsfolk of Dirtwood formed a posse, arrested him and threw him into Beaver Ridge jail to rot. For seven long years Luke plotted his revenge and then he finally managed to escape. Now he could act out his vengeance!

But when he rides into Dirtwood, the town is already in the grip of fear. Josh Carter and his ruthless outlaw gang have taken over the town and only Luke's childhood friend Ethan Craig has the courage to stand up to them.

Luke readily adds to Dirtwood's woes, but as the lead flies and the bodies mount, can an old friendship offer a man as murderous as Luke one last chance of redemption?

Bad Day in Dirtwood

I. J. Parnham

A Black Horse Western

ROBERT HALE · LONDON

© I. J. Parnham 2003
First published in Great Britain 2003

ISBN 0 7090 7360 7

Robert Hale Limited
Clerkenwell House
Clerkenwell Green
London EC1R 0HT

Typeset by
Derek Doyle & Associates, Liverpool.
Printed and bound in Great Britain by
Antony Rowe Limited, Wiltshire

CHAPTER 1

Ethan Craig sauntered into the saloon, while his friend, Wiley Douglas, kept two paces back.

Scattered about the saloon were around half of Josh Carter's men. Josh leaned against the back wall with his hired gun, Vince McGiven, watching a poker-game with a leg raised so that the flat of his boot rested on the wall.

Ethan stood before the bar. 'Whiskey,' he muttered.

The bartender, Doc Taylor, looked up and winced.

'You know I can't serve you, Ethan,' he said with a sigh. 'But take a few words of advice. Josh ain't seen you yet, so leave.'

Wiley slipped closer to the bar and patted Ethan's shoulder. 'Doc is talking sense. We don't need a drink *that* bad. Let's go before there's trouble.'

Ethan shrugged. 'I'm staying so there *is* trouble.'

'Yeah, that's what I was afraid of – and it's coming.'

Ethan turned. Josh Carter was striding across the saloon, his fists clenching and unclenching. He loomed over Ethan and glared at Doc.

'Why are you serving Ethan?' Josh muttered. 'I told you he ain't welcome.'

Doc gulped. 'I was explaining that to him.'

Josh rolled his tongue around his lips and spat on Ethan's boots.

'If our bartender has explained your role in life, why are you still here?'

'I want a drink,' Ethan said, providing his best smile.

As Josh narrowed his eyes to streaks of ice, Ethan glanced to the door.

A man stood in the doorway. His face was chiselled and a star gleamed on his jacket. With his legs set wide he stared around the saloon.

Ethan smiled at Doc. 'So as I was saying – I'll have a whiskey, and so will my old friend Wiley and so will my new friend Sheriff Quinn Ogden.'

In the doorway Sheriff Ogden rummaged in his pocket. He pulled out a match, lit it on the sole of his boot, and tapped the end to a half-smoked cheroot. He blew out a puff of smoke and swaggered to the bar.

'You folks wait outside,' he said. 'I'll take care of this.'

Ethan sighed. 'Can't go. I ain't had my drink yet.'

Wiley nudged Ethan in the ribs. 'Ethan, you heard the sheriff.'

'Yeah,' Ethan said, 'but this affects us more than anybody.'

'But we ain't armed.'

'If you're worried, go, but I'm staying.'

Wiley glanced at Sheriff Ogden, then dashed for the swing-doors.

Ogden watched Wiley go. Then he leaned on the bar and stared at the rows of whiskey bottles opposite.

Rock Forrest, one of the least ornery of Josh's men, pushed back from his poker-game and sidled along

6

the wall towards the door.

Without turning, Ogden coughed.

'You by the wall, stay there and tell me where I can find Josh Carter.'

'Josh is—' Ethan said, but Ogden lifted a hand, silencing him.

'I asked *this* man that question.'

'Why do you want to see Josh?' Rock asked, glancing at Josh.

Keeping his movements slow, Ogden turned. He glared at Rock, appraising him from scuffed boots to frayed hat. He smiled.

'Don't recognize you, but then again I don't remember the worthless troublemakers.' He glanced around the saloon. 'That'd include Josh Carter too.'

'Right, Sheriff,' Josh muttered, baring his yellow teeth and drawing himself to his full height. 'You have my attention. What do you want?'

Ogden flicked away his cheroot and ground it into the floor.

'Can see why *you* kept quiet. Ugly critter like you can't want too many people knowing he exists.'

Doc chuckled, then silenced as Josh flashed him a harsh glare.

'You ain't funny,' Josh said, 'even for a lawman.'

Ogden folded his arms. 'Let's get to it, Josh. You've some questions to answer.'

'Say your piece, Sheriff.'

'You and your boys have made Dirtwood your new home. That's fine, but this is a hardworking town and you're keen on trouble. You've done nothing that I can't put down to high spirits, so let's keep it that way. It's time to move on.'

Josh nodded. 'Sounds reasonable.'

'Glad to hear it. I thought you'd see sense when the law arrived.' Ogden tipped his hat. 'I'm having a drink with Ethan. Your men can finish their drinks too and then be on their way.'

'We'll go, but Ethan ain't drinking in here.'

Ogden shrugged. He swung round and ordered a bottle of whiskey.

Doc glanced at Josh, then placed a whiskey bottle and a single glass on the bar.

With a sigh, Ogden grabbed a dirty glass from further down the bar. He wiped it on his sleeve and poured two generous measures of whiskey.

'Both those drinks had better be for yourself, Sheriff,' Josh muttered.

'And if they ain't?'

Josh smiled. Without warning, he twitched his arm, his gun coming to hand and spewing lead three times, each shot a moment apart.

Faced with the hail of bullets, Ogden spun back and around, his half-pulled weapon catching on his holster. He collapsed against the bar and slid to the floor.

With an arrogant twirl of his hand, Josh put a final bullet in the sheriff's forehead.

The body rose and collapsed, then lay still.

'I was going to say that if both drinks ain't for you, you won't like the result,' Josh muttered. He smiled at Ethan.

Ethan gulped and edged along the bar. He glanced at his escape route through the swing-doors. Outside,

Josh's brother, Farley, dashed across the road from Peter's store, the remainder of Josh's men behind him. They barged into the saloon.

'Remove that mess, Farley,' Josh shouted. 'And next time, get here quicker.'

'Who is he?' Farley said, looking at the body.

Josh tapped a boot against the sheriff's side. 'Some man with a star.'

Farley sighed. 'This is serious, Josh. You can't shoot a lawman.'

With a casual shrug, Josh leaned on the bar.

Ethan hung his head as Farley and Rock dragged the sheriff's body back across the saloon. When they were outside, he filed after them.

'Wait!' Josh shouted.

Ethan kept walking but rapid footsteps sounded and a firm hand slammed on his shoulder. Still keeping his eyes down, he turned.

'What's wrong?'

Josh gripped his hand tighter. 'I'm asking myself why a lawman came to the god-forsaken town of Dirtwood to buy you a drink.'

Ethan shrugged. 'Lawmen do that sort of thing.'

'That ain't the answer.'

Ethan squirmed, removing Josh's hand from his shoulder.

'Believe what you want.'

'Don't want belief. I want an answer.' Josh snapped his fingers and three of his men took a long pace towards Ethan. 'And you're the man who'll give it to me.'

*

'I ain't returning.'

'We ain't,' Luke McCoy said, running a hand through his blond hair. He nodded to Ron Jameson and sighed. 'No matter what.'

Ron patted the third member of their group, Wesley Jameson, on the shoulder.

'You did well getting us this far, Wesley. No reason to get you killed too. You can walk out of here. Luke and I will take our chances.'

Wesley glanced over the windowsill, then dropped to the floor.

'Thanks for the offer,' Wesley said, 'but I ain't leaving my younger brother.'

'Yeah, but—'

'Stop!' Luke shouted. 'We ain't got time for family discussions. Wesley helped us escape. Even if he gives himself up, he'll face a few years behind bars. If he don't want that, it's his choice.'

Ron shrugged and wiped his sweating forehead.

'Suppose you're right. What are we doing, then?'

Luke bent his tall form and sidled along the floor. He joined Wesley by the window and glanced outside.

Facing them were Marshal Foster and three deputies. For a week, these men had pursued them since they'd escaped from Beaver Ridge jail.

They had been relentless.

Wesley was a trapper and knew how to cover tracks and confuse a pursuer. None of his tricks had confused these men for long and now they had forced them to make their stand in an abandoned house with one gun and a handful of bullets between them.

Foster stood apart from his three deputies, his rifle resting across one arm.

'Come out!' he roared. 'This is your last warning. It's your choice whether I return with your hides strung over your horses or in chains.'

Ron spat on the floor. 'Don't look like we're leaving here alive, but that marshal ain't leaving either.'

Luke snorted. 'He's an irritating son of a bitch and that's official.'

'What's it to be?' Foster shouted.

'Go to hell!' Luke shouted, lifting his head to the window.

Ron nodded. With his gun raised to shoulder height, he stood three paces back from the door.

'I'll take the first man that comes through the door,' he said, wiping sweat from his forehead. 'After that, we'll need luck.'

Luke sighed as he appraised Ron's stance. Ron was shaking, the gun barrel roving in a circle.

'I have a better plan,' Luke said.

Ron sighed. 'Then don't keep it to yourself. Any second now they'll come through that door.'

Luke held out a hand. 'Give me the gun.'

Ron narrowed his eyes. 'I'll only release this gun when I'm dead.'

'Which is in about ten seconds. I have the better chance.'

As Ron shook his head, Wesley stood.

'Luke might be talking sense, Ron,' he said. 'He claims to be a fast hand. Perhaps we should let him prove it.'

Ron frowned. 'We've only Luke's word for his skills.'

Luke mimed pulling a gun. 'You know I have fast

11

reflexes. Give me the gun.'

Ron firmed his gun towards the door.

'Ain't seen a fast draw before. Can't judge if you're right, except in action, and then it'll be too late.'

Wesley glanced through the window. The men were fanning out and closing in.

'We'll die if you have the gun, Ron. Luke might be wrong, but I reckon he's our only chance. I'd sooner take a chance on living than die.'

Ron spat to the side and opened his mouth as if to shout his refusal. Then he lowered his head. He let the gun barrel swing down, then threw the gun to Luke.

In a casual gesture, Luke caught the gun one-handed and hefted it, getting used to the weight. It'd been some years since he'd held a weapon and the cold metal sent a flurry of anticipation surging through his veins.

From his pocket, Ron pulled out their four spare bullets, but Luke shook his head.

'Only four men are out there,' Luke said. 'I hit what I aim at. If I live long enough to take them, I won't need those bullets.'

Ron sighed. 'Hope that confidence ain't misplaced.'

Luke stood and flexed his shoulders. He tucked the gun in his belt and rubbed his fingers on his jacket, removing the sweat.

'It ain't. Trust me and we'll walk away.'

Wesley nodded and a few seconds later, Ron nodded too. Luke took a deep breath.

'Marshal,' he shouted. 'We've been talking and we're coming out.'

'You've been talking sense,' Foster shouted from close to.

Luke turned to Wesley. 'Are they in the open?'

Wesley peered through the window. 'They're right before the door.'

'That's the last mistake they'll make.'

'Come out one at a time,' Foster shouted. 'When you come through the door, put your hands high and walk real slow or you'll be spitting bullets.'

'We know the drill, Marshal,' Luke shouted.

Luke strode to the door and flung it wide. With his hands raised to his shoulders, he stood a moment. Framed through the doorway he saw their four pursuers spread out before the house.

With his rifle to his shoulder, Foster stood before the three deputies. The barrel was still as it aimed at Luke's forehead.

The three deputies stood hunched with guns drawn and centred on Luke.

'Put those hands higher,' Foster muttered.

Luke raised his hands above his head and took a long pace.

'This high enough?'

Foster paced sideways towards the house, keeping his rifle on Luke. 'It'll do.'

'What's next, Marshal?'

Five yards to Luke's left, Foster stopped his pacing.

'You have a gun, so listen. Unarmed men can live the rest of their worthless lives in prison. Armed men can die. You have five seconds to decide which kind of man you'd rather be.'

Luke took a long pace from the house into the sunlight. He looked around the arc of deputies.

'If those are the choices, I'll be an unarmed man.'

'You're a wise man. Place your thumb and finger on the stock and pull out the gun real slow. The first sudden movement will be your last.'

'I'll be as slow as you want, Marshal.'

With his left hand, Luke rubbed the sweat from his forehead. Then he extended his thumb and index finger wide. He edged his hand to his belt and gripped the stock. He pulled, the gun inching above his belt.

Foster firmed his rifle. 'If you keep moving that slow, you'll be fine.'

When the barrel cleared his belt and the gun swung free, Luke smiled.

'Do you want me to drop the gun or throw it to you?'

'Drop the gun and take three paces. Then lie face down and place your hands behind your back.'

Luke nodded and swung his arm up six inches. He stared at the deputy furthest to his right. Then he dropped the gun.

In a move like lightning, Luke thrust his shoulders down.

Foster fired. The slug blasted Luke's hat from his head as he plummeted.

Before the gun hit the ground, Luke grabbed it with his right hand and swung it up. With a reflex series of deft movements, he fired, winging Foster with a gunshot to the hip.

Luke hit the ground and rolled, gunfire blasting around him. He came up on one knee and three crisp shots ripped from his gun, each less than a heartbeat apart and each taking the deputies through their chests. Each man spun away.

Before any of the men hit the ground, Luke swung

the gun back to Foster and put a second bullet in his forehead.

Then he leapt to his feet.

From behind him, Ron and Wesley dashed from the house and slid to a halt.

Ron threw down his hat and danced a jig around it.

'Well I'll be . . .' he shouted. He whistled through his teeth. 'You ain't just talk. You can shoot like no man I've seen.'

Luke smiled. 'Told you before that you should've given me the gun. If you had, we wouldn't have spent the last week having these men after us.'

Ron shrugged. He wandered to the deputies' bodies and checked that each man was dead.

'Looks like we're free men. It's been a while.'

Luke nodded and stood over Foster's body. He underhanded Ron's gun back to him. With his boot, he rolled the marshal over and slipped out his gunbelt. He wrapped the belt around his waist and rolled his hips, letting the belt slip down.

With his long legs set wide, he rubbed his hands.

'What you going to do now, Ron?'

'Don't know,' Ron said, scratching his head. 'Got so many choices, it's hard to decide. Guess I know what your first choice will be.'

'What's that then?'

'That cool glass of whiskey you've been talking about for the last few years. Sometimes reckon that thinking about that drink is the only thing that's kept you alive.'

'Sometimes reckon that myself. Trouble is I reckon that anticipating that drink might be better than the drink.'

Ron laughed and grabbed the nearest horse's reins. He glanced at Wesley, who nodded.

'We're heading east,' Wesley said. 'You're welcome to ride with us.'

'Nope,' Luke said. 'We'll do better if we split up and anyhow, I'm heading west.'

As Wesley jumped on to his horse, Ron shrugged.

'Any particular place?' he asked.

'Yeah. A town called Dirtwood.'

Ron swung into the saddle too. He chuckled. 'Sounds nice.'

'Used to be.' Luke spat on the ground. 'That won't last.'

Ron tipped his hat. 'We need to be far enough away before the next pursuit begins. When it comes, it'll be more serious. If you remember those tricks Wesley taught us and avoid trouble, you should be fine.'

'I probably won't be fine then.'

'Even so, good luck.' Ron laughed. 'Always reckoned it'd be fun to have a price on my head. What do you reckon the price will be?'

Luke shrugged. 'A hundred dollars or so for us two . . . perhaps less for Wesley.'

Wesley sighed. 'Nobody knows I helped you escape. I won't have a price. They'll only look for you two.'

To suppress a smile Luke bit his lip.

'You shouldn't have put that idea in my head.'

'What idea?'

'Ignore me. I'm thinking about that drink again.'

Ron and Wesley provided another cheery wave, then turned.

When they'd ridden twenty yards, Luke lifted his gun

and fired two slugs into Wesley's and Ron's backs.

Both men tumbled from their horses and landed in a cloud of dust.

In a few long paces Luke strode to Wesley's body. He confirmed that he wasn't breathing, but he'd hit Ron lower in the back and he writhed in agony.

'Why did . . . we were . . . we were friends,' Ron said between pain-racked gasps.

'Sorry, Ron. We were. Except friends can turn on you as much as your enemies.' Luke frowned. 'Besides, I need two bodies. They'd be yours and mine.'

Luke put a bullet in Ron's forehead. Then he dragged the six bodies into the house and riffled through everyone's pockets. He arranged three bodies by the door and scattered the other three across the room. He collected dry branches from out back. Working quickly, he bunched the branches around the doorway and piled the remaining wood inside.

The marshal had a knife so Luke struck sparks from a stone and started a fire. Once the fire had taken hold he stood back while it built into an inferno.

Luke let the heat warm him, ensuring that it'd be hot enough to destroy the building and mask the bodies' identities. Then he jumped on his horse and swung it round.

When he left the house, he headed west, his pace untroubled.

CHAPTER 2

Farley Carter lifted his fist again.

'Who called for the lawman?' he screamed.

Ethan spat a stream of blood on the floor.

'Told you before. I called for him.'

Farley flexed his hand and nodded to Rock and Davis who were holding Ethan's arms behind his back.

'Start telling me the truth, before I stop holding back.'

Ethan grinned. 'Go to hell, Farley.'

With a grunt, Farley swung his fist back and slammed it into Ethan's guts.

Although Ethan had tensed, the wind blasted from him and he had to gulp to stop himself retching over his boots.

'Tell me,' Farley roared. 'When I stop holding back, you'll break in half.'

Ethan cleared his throat. He shook away the blood that was running into his eyes and glared at Farley.

'I've told you everything. Three weeks ago I left Dirtwood and went to Hail Ridge. I got word to someone there. He fetched Sheriff Ogden.'

'And the name of the someone in Hail Ridge?'

With his eyes narrowed, Ethan smiled. 'I don't remember.'

Farley chuckled. 'Let's see if I can remind you.'

Farley flexed his fist, then hammered it deep into Ethan's guts.

The blow knocked back Ethan and the men holding him, and he slipped from their grip and fell to the floor. Finding he was free, Ethan tried to rise but he couldn't force his arms to push him upright. He glared at Farley.

'Ain't remembered yet,' he muttered.

'Let's start from the beginning.' Farley waved to Davis who hauled Ethan to his feet. 'This time—'

'Wait!' someone shouted from the doorway.

Everyone turned as Wiley Douglas strode into the saloon.

'Leave, Wiley,' Farley muttered. 'Me and Ethan have some serious talking to do.'

'Except Ethan ain't telling you how we got word to Sheriff Ogden.'

'Don't,' Ethan cried.

Farley swung round and slapped Ethan across the face with the back of his hand.

'Quiet. Wiley is about to start talking sense.' Farley turned back to Wiley and nodded. 'Go on.'

'It was me,' Wiley said, holding his chin high. 'Ethan had nothing to do with Sheriff Ogden coming here and neither did anyone else in Dirtwood. *I* went to Hail Ridge. A rancher was passing through. I gave him a letter to deliver to Stone Creek asking Sheriff Ogden to come and help us. The rest you know.'

Farley shrugged. 'That tale is pretty much the same as Ethan's. I wonder why?'

19

'Because it's the truth. Only difference is – I did the writing. If you have a problem with that, take it out on me, but Ethan is innocent.'

Farley glanced at his red-rimmed knuckles. He spat on his hand and rubbed away some of the blood.

'Guessed so,' he murmured. 'Not all of the blood is Ethan's. I need to give my fist a rest.'

Josh chuckled. 'Yeah. It's my turn to find the truth. You can't have all the fun.'

Josh spun on his heel and sauntered behind the bar. He wandered back, clutching a bullwhip.

Wiley's eyes opened wide and he gulped.

'You can't do that. I did what I had to do.'

Josh unfurled the whip and smiled. He grunted orders and Rock dashed behind the bar. He emerged with a long rope. As he tied Wiley's hands, Wiley didn't resist but glanced at Ethan and shook his head.

Rock threw the rope over a beam in the ceiling. He hauled back, pulling Wiley's arms above his head so that he had to stand on tiptoes. Then he attached the rope to a cupboard behind the bar and returned to helping Davis hold Ethan.

'Farley explained how this works to Ethan,' Josh said, clearing a wide area around Wiley. 'But Ethan didn't understand and he received some bruises. You're brighter than he is. After all, you thought of fetching help. Ain't that so?'

'Yeah,' Wiley whispered, glancing at Ethan who closed his eyes.

'Good, because whenever you tell me something I don't believe, this happens.'

Josh swirled the whip. It cracked and swung around

20

Wiley's chest flaying a slice of cloth from his shirt.

Wiley screamed, then hung his head.

'I'll tell you the truth, no trouble, no trouble at all,' he babbled.

'So tell me the truth. When did you decide to fetch a lawman?' Josh rolled his shoulders and backed a pace.

Wiley flexed his shoulders and took a deep breath.

'When you started saying who could use the saloon. That wasn't right.'

Josh walked in a circle nodding. He looked up.

'I believe you. Why did you go to Hail Ridge?'

Wiley sighed. 'The nearest trail back east goes through Hail Ridge.'

Josh nodded. 'Believe that too. Who did you discuss your plans with?'

'Nobody.'

The whip cracked and Wiley cried out.

'Think again,' Josh whispered, his voice loud in the sudden silence.

Ethan hung his head further. Behind him his captors relaxed as they chuckled and grinned at each other. Then with his weight set forward, Ethan slammed his heel back into Davis's shin.

To grab his hurt leg Davis released Ethan's arm.

Ethan ripped his left arm from Rock's grip and hammered his right elbow into Rock's stomach. As Rock staggered back, he spun round and slammed the flat of his hand against his chin, flooring him.

Seeing Farley dashing across the saloon to him, Ethan dropped to the floor and pushed Rock over, scrambling his hands along his gunbelt, but before he reached the gun, Davis leapt on his back. He threw Davis over his shoulder, but tumbled himself to the floor with the effort. As he rose, Farley's boot slammed into his temple.

Disorientated, Ethan rolled back and staggered to his feet. To clear his vision he shook his head, but Farley's fist thundered into his chin and blasted all strength from his body. He tumbled over. His head hit the floor and he lay, unable to move.

Farley dragged Ethan's hands behind his back but he couldn't stay conscious, the blackness closing on him.

'Wiley,' Josh shouted. 'Tell me again. Who did you discuss your plans with?'

'Nobody,' Wiley muttered.

The whip cracked, but the sound was distant to Ethan as he slipped into unconsciousness.

Ethan's vision stayed dark. Occasionally, he almost dragged himself back to consciousness, but he couldn't move. A steady crack of the whip echoed through his troubled dreams.

Minutes or hours passed. Then Ethan shook his head and blinked, realizing that he was awake. His vision focused on Wiley's glistening body dangling from the ceiling. Ethan gulped and looked away.

Five yards back, Josh flexed his bullwhip and stretched his arms.

With a sickness in his gut, Ethan staggered to his feet. Nobody stopped him.

On the other side of the saloon Josh's men sat around the tables chatting and grinning at what was happening to Wiley.

Ethan took a deep breath and staggered to Wiley's side. So much blood coated Wiley's body that he saw no way to help him. With a shaking hand, he placed two fingers under Wiley's chin and lifted his head.

Under Ethan's hand Wiley's heavy head lolled. He gripped the chin harder and stared into Wiley's blank eyes.

'Move, Ethan,' Josh muttered. 'Still got more questions to ask Wiley.'

As Josh unfurled the whip, Ethan shook his head.

'You ain't getting any more answers from Wiley. He's long dead.'

Josh smirked. 'He's resting. I'll soon wake him.'

'You won't,' Ethan muttered. He rolled forward ready to leap at Josh and beat his revenge from him or die in the attempt.

Then with a whirl of his arm, Josh cracked the whip. The whip hurtled towards Wiley's dangling body.

Ethan grabbed the whip. Ignoring the intense stinging pain, he wrapped it around his hand and tugged.

Josh braced himself and tugged back.

'Let go or I'll start asking you those questions.'

'You can, but you ain't flogging a dead man.'

Josh glared back, then gestured to the bar.

Doc came from behind the bar and examined Wiley. He backed, nodding.

'Ethan is right,' he whispered. 'Wiley is dead.'

Ethan threw down his end of the whip and stormed to the back of the bar. He untied the end of the rope. Keeping his movements slow, he lowered Wiley to the floor.

As the entertainment was over everyone else grouped at the back of the saloon and chatted.

With his eyes downcast, Ethan strode from behind the bar and untied Wiley. Blood poured over his hands as he hoisted Wiley into his arms and dragged him towards the door.

'Wait!' Josh shouted.

Ethan took another pace towards the door. In his weakened state he staggered from the weight. The whip cracked around his chest and he dropped to his knees. Wiley spilled from his arms.

He pushed to his feet and again slipped his hands under Wiley's back.

'I said wait!' Josh roared.

Rock kicked Ethan to the floor and Davis dragged him from Wiley.

'You can't do anything more to him,' Ethan shouted.

'Ain't worried about him no more.' Josh pointed at Wiley's body. 'Farley, hang him outside the saloon.'

'Why?' Ethan whispered as Farley and two other men bundled Wiley outside. 'This is too barbaric even for you.'

'It's a warning.' Josh grinned. 'The rest of your towns-folk need to know who's in charge – and that's me.'

Ethan winced. He took long breaths until the men had cleared outside. Then he shrugged his jacket closed, turned on his heel, and strode on to the boardwalk.

A huddle of townsfolk stood across the road watching Josh's men drag Wiley from the saloon. As they strung him up, the townsfolk removed their hats and lowered their heads in silent respect.

Ethan ignored them and strode to his cart. Each of his many bruises complained as he climbed on it. With an angry crack of the reins, he swung the cart round and headed down the road.

The only two mounted townsfolk, Felix and Sam, cantered to him and drew alongside.

'You need help?' Felix asked.

'I'm fine,' Ethan muttered, gazing to the darkened fields beyond the end of the road.

'You have an awful lot of blood on—'

'It ain't all mine,' Ethan snapped. Then he took a long breath. 'I'm sorry. They killed Wiley just for fetching the sheriff.'

Felix sighed. 'Know it ain't the time to say this, but I said he was wrong to fetch a lawman.'

Ethan pulled back on the reins, drawing the cart to a halt. He spat on the ground.

'You're right. This ain't the time to say that.'

Felix gulped. 'I know you, Ethan. You'll do something and make things even worse.'

'Things can't get worse.'

'They can,' Felix whispered. 'Josh is a weak troublemaker. He's probably sounding tough, but he ain't stupid. He'll run like the dog he is. Then the rest of us can rebuild our lives. Don't push him any further.'

'And what about justice?'

'It'll come. Men like Josh can't avoid that for ever.'

Ethan glanced back at Wiley's body, which swung back and forth before the saloon.

'Creatures like Josh only understand one rule. As he's got a taste for killing, he won't stop with the lawman and Wiley.'

Ethan stared at Felix, who with the barest movement shook his head.

'Please, Ethan. Don't do anything stupid.'

Ethan sneered and cracked the reins, hurtling the cart out of Dirtwood and back to his farm.

He didn't look back.

CHAPTER 3

'You sitting at that table all morning?' Martha asked. She was sitting by the hearth, dressing the children, Dale and Sarah.

Ethan shrugged. 'Might do.'

'Then you can get them ready and I'll start the chores.'

Ethan slammed his hands on his legs and stood.

'I understand. I'll stop moping.'

'It'd help.' Martha sighed and put her hands on her hips. 'I'm concerned about what happened to Wiley and that poor sheriff too, but life has to go on.'

Ethan stretched his back, freeing a twinge from yesterday's beating. With both hands, he tousled each of his children's hair and laughed.

'Tended to forget plenty of things recently. I'm sorry, but—'

'I know what you're going to say. But your family comes first. Putting yourself in front will get you killed too. Then what will we do?' Martha lowered her voice. 'These children have lost one ma. I doubt they could cope with losing a pa too.'

To avoid offering ill-considered words Ethan bit his lip, then strode to the window. He threw wide the shutters.

'That's why I did what I did. I put you first and if that means risking my life, so be it.'

'We don't want you to die, whatever the reason.'

'Wiley had no folks, but if he had, I guess they wouldn't have wanted him to do what he did either. But he died without saying who helped him.' Ethan slammed his fist into his hand. 'I ain't forgetting that loyalty.'

Martha gulped. 'Felix was right. You *are* going to do something stupid.'

As Martha shooed the children outside Ethan turned on his heel and faced her.

'When did you speak to Felix?'

When the children were outside, Martha rolled to her feet.

'He came last night. I didn't wake you. You'd been through enough. At the last town meeting he said you were full of damn-fool plans to run Josh out of town and only Wiley agreed with any of them. As fetching that lawman has failed, he reckons you won't listen to reason.'

Ethan smiled. 'Felix knows me better than I thought.'

'Whatever you're thinking about doing, don't.'

Ethan stared at Martha, then turned to the window. Outside, Dale and Sarah were flicking clods of earth at each other and giggling.

'I'll do whatever it takes to protect my own.'

'You ain't the only one with a say in this.'

Still with his back turned, Ethan sighed.

'I know. You have a right to an opinion, and I'll be careful. If I was on my own, I'd do things differently, but with you to consider, I'll ensure I get out of this alive.'

Martha strode across the room. She placed a hand on his shoulder and joined him in watching their children.

'I didn't mean that. I'll go along with what you think is best. You wouldn't get yourself killed, but I worry about the rest of the town.'

Ethan chuckled. 'I can take care of Felix.'

Martha gripped her hand tighter. 'Despite what you think, Felix doesn't run Dirtwood. But he represents everyone's feelings and nobody wants this to escalate. They want to ride it out. Josh is the kind of man that roves about. He'll go somewhere else soon.'

'Expected to hear that sort of talk from Felix, but not from you. As long as another town suffers, we're supposed to turn our backs, are we?'

'You know I didn't mean that. You going off on your own might not get *you* killed, but it could get others killed.'

With his right hand, Ethan patted Martha's hand. 'I know.'

'We have a town meeting at the end of the week. Felix said you're to do nothing until then and whatever the town decides you must go along with it.' Martha rolled her hand round to squeeze Ethan's hand. 'I agree.'

Ethan sighed and lifted Martha's hand to her side. He leaned a moment beside the window, shaking his head.

'And if I ain't happy with those rules?'

'He said you should stay away from the meeting.'

Ethan chuckled and strode to the door past Martha.

'Sometimes what Felix wants and what I want coincide.'

'What does that mean?' Martha shouted as Ethan opened the door.

Keeping his back turned, Ethan strode outside.

His eldest, Dale, sat outside, picking dirt from his hair.

Ethan tousled his blond hair again. Then he strode to his barn.

Three days after Wiley's death, Cooper Rodgers strode across the fields towards Ethan.

Ethan stretched his aching back, the bruising still hurting him, and watched Cooper's steady progress.

When Cooper reached his side, he tipped his hat.

'Howdy, Ethan. Peter said you wanted me.'

'I do.'

Cooper looked around. 'You have a fine spread here.'

'I have. Intend to ensure it stays that way.'

Cooper smiled. 'We need to talk about how we ensure you do that.'

Ethan nodded. 'Wondered when you'd ask.'

With a wide grin, Cooper ushered Ethan to his cart.

They'd ridden a good few miles along the trail before Cooper coughed.

'Your family happy about you leaving?'

Ethan allowed the cart's steady rhythm to jostle him. Behind him the bags of provisions rustled. He turned to Cooper.

'Martha reckons I ain't been much use around the

farm for the last few weeks. She can handle things better than I can now.'

Cooper sighed. 'I didn't mean that.'

'I know.'

Cooper took a deep breath. 'You realize I have no proof he's still there? Been a good month since I last passed through Hail Ridge.'

'Yup.'

'And you realize that I ain't heading back this way afterwards?'

'Yup. I know you're a businessman and you have your duties.'

'Just so we're clear.'

They rode in silence. Then Ethan sighed.

'You're taking a big risk in taking me to Hail Ridge.'

'I know. I also know that Wiley died without telling Josh that I helped him, so I owe him and everyone else to help again.'

'We're much obliged.'

'From what I've heard, most people reckon this is a bad idea.'

Ethan nodded. 'In that case, *I* am much obliged.'

'Don't thank me. Trade was better before Josh arrived. Just trying to return to those days.'

'I know what you're doing and that ain't the whole truth.'

Cooper smiled. 'Reckon what you like but you're taking the bigger gamble. I ain't got a family, but what will happen to yours if Josh realizes that you've headed out of town?'

Ethan rubbed his chin, feeling the soreness under the skin.

'Sam will look out for them, and anyhow, Farley gave me a good beating. When Josh doesn't see me, he'll reckon I'm being sensible and lying low. Before someone notices I ain't around, I'll be back.'

'Except you'll have company.'

Ethan grunted. 'And this man won't follow the rules.'

After a week of steady riding, Farley Carter and Big Dawson rode into Hard Creek and headed straight for the sheriff's office.

Farley stretched his back and jumped from the cart. He told Dawson to stay outside, then strode into the office. Once inside, he forced himself to smile as he faced Sheriff Irons.

'Howdy, Sheriff,' he said.

Without moving his feet from his desk, Irons shrugged.

'Howdy.'

Farley slipped his hat from his head and held it low.

'Got something outside you ought to see.'

Irons clattered his feet down from his desk. He sauntered past Farley and stood on the boardwalk.

'I'm out here. What should I see?'

Farley strode to the cart. He battered Dawson's hat from his head and stood by the back of the cart. With Dawson's help, he lifted the cloth that covered the back and nodded to the two bodies that lay beneath.

Irons wrinkled his nose at the ripe odour and wafted away a cloud of flies.

'Suppose I'm obliged to you for bringing them in. But burying them where you'd found them would have been better.'

31

'Yeah, perhaps we should have, but I thought I ought to bring them here.'

Irons shrugged and jumped on to the cart. He narrowed his eyes. With his face averted, he pulled the star from the jacket of one of the bodies. He glanced at Farley.

Farley nodded. 'That's why I brought them in.'

Irons returned the nod. He jumped from the cart and ordered Dawson to take the cart across the road to the undertaker's workshop. Then he beckoned Farley to follow him into his office.

Irons sat behind his desk and clattered his legs on the top.

'You'd better tell me how Sheriff Ogden died.'

Farley folded his arms. 'A gang of ruffians headed by Wiley Douglas roared into Dirtwood – a town out West. He shot up the place and took over the saloon. Dawson, the man who went to your undertaker, got word to Stone Creek that we needed help and Sheriff Ogden arrived.'

'He's a good lawman.'

'He is. Within an hour, he'd run the ruffians out of town, but Wiley Douglas ain't happy. He returned and called the sheriff from the saloon. Wiley shot the sheriff before he could square up to him. Never seen anything like it.' Farley sighed. 'The sheriff tried to help us and Wiley filled him with bullets for his trouble.'

Irons sighed. 'Yeah, I saw that too.'

'We planned to take his body back to Stone Creek, but that's another week away and so we stopped here.' Farley held his nose and winced.

32

'After a week on the trail the smell is bad enough. You did right and I'll be grateful for your help in finding this Wiley Douglas.'

'No need.' Farley smiled. 'I have Wiley for you too. He's the other body in the cart.'

'How did he die?'

'It's a bit of a tale,' Farley said, glancing around.

Irons shrugged. 'I have no problem with Wiley being dead. The body was ripe but I saw the signs. That lawman-killer died on the end of a rope and suffered too.'

'He did, but we ain't proud of what we done.'

'You did nothing to be ashamed of. Ain't many lawmen out here. You townsfolk have to defend yourself anyway you see fit.'

'Thanks, Sheriff. I'm sure our townsfolk will be mighty pleased to hear that you think that way.'

Irons stood and sauntered to a list of names on the wall, where some prominent faces stood out from the wanted posters.

'Ogden was a fast draw. Surprised I ain't heard of this Wiley Douglas if he could take the sheriff. You reckon he was from out of state?'

'He had a Texan drawl.'

Irons nodded. 'Might explain why I ain't heard of him. How did you get him?'

'The sheriff *was* a fast draw, except Wiley attacked him before he was ready, but even then, the sheriff got a shot back and winged him. We charged Wiley and before he knew what was happening, we had him trussed like the animal he was.'

'Guess he didn't like what happened next?'

Farley wrapped his hands around his neck and mimed screaming.

'You guessed right.'

'You reckon as you'll have no trouble from the other hardcases?'

Farley grinned. 'No chance. They ran when we attacked Wiley. After we'd strung him up, we scouted around but they were long gone. Dirtwood won't see trouble again, not when we folks have learnt to defend ourselves. Town spirit is as high as it's ever been.'

Irons nodded. 'Glad to hear it. As I have no details on this Wiley, there's no reward. Might be one when I get word back from Texas.'

Farley shrugged. 'Wasn't looking for a reward, just a town free of his type.'

'I guessed as much. Dirtwood sounds a fine place with fine people.'

'Yup.' Farley tipped his hat. 'I'll leave, Sheriff. I'm heading to the saloon to get some whiskey inside me. After a week riding at the front of that cart, the smell will take a while to clear.'

'You do that.' Irons extracted two coins from his pocket. 'Ain't much, but have a drink on me to the sheriff's name. He was a good man.'

'I will.'

Farley grabbed the coins. He tipped his hat and strode outside. He stopped on the boardwalk, licking his lips. A grin emerged.

'Idiot,' he whispered.

Eight drinks after arriving in the saloon, Big Dawson was as cheerful as he ever was.

'So,' he shouted, 'you want to hear the story again, do you?'

A round of agreement from the saloon folk thundered in Farley's ears. Farley sighed. Dawson had told the story through twice and the gossip-starved drinkers were still enthusiastic for more.

He sidled along the bar to Dawson.

'We need to head back. Got a few days' journey ahead of us.'

'Then it don't matter if we stay a while longer.' Dawson leaned on Farley to avoid falling over as the saloon folk offered a round of support. 'Except I'm too dry to tell the tale again.'

Two whiskeys arrived and a full bottle skidded to a halt beside Dawson a few moments later.

'This enough?' an eager drinker asked.

Dawson swayed towards the whiskeys, grinning.

Farley grabbed Dawson's arm as he reached for the nearest whiskey.

'I made a big mistake in giving Wiley's real name,' Farley whispered. 'The more people you tell this tale to, the more chance we'll meet someone who knows the real Wiley.'

'Wiley's a common name.' Dawson slipped his arm from under Farley's grip and grabbed the drink.

'Even so, I'll tell the tale this time. You might forget some details.'

'Never,' Dawson shouted and knocked back two whiskeys in quick succession. 'I'm remembering more details with every drink.'

Farley sighed. 'Yeah, that's what worries me.'

'Anyhow,' Dawson shouted and spun round to face

his attentive audience. He swayed to a halt and grinned. 'It was six weeks ago that Wiley Douglas rode into town. He was the roughest varmint I'd ever clapped eyes on. His eyes were close together, his gun-hand never strayed far from his hip, and the only thing on his mind was trouble.'

Dawson poured a drink and gulped it down.

From the back of the crowd of eager listeners, a tall, blond-haired man paced a long step from the group.

'This Wiley Douglas,' the tall man said. 'Did he ride into Dirtwood?'

'He did,' Dawson shouted. 'He was the meanest varmint in the West. If you ain't heard my tale, settle down and hear what he did to our town.'

Farley appraised this new man, who had the rangy look of one who had seen hard times, but revelled in them. The man nodded to each of Dawson's invented descriptions of Wiley.

When Dawson finished, the tall man folded his arms and nodded.

'That sounds like the Wiley Douglas I'd heard about. He's as mean as they come and then some. I'll have a drink and hear what happened to him.'

'You do that,' Dawson slurred and returned to his tale.

Farley stopped listening to Dawson and watched the tall man stride to the bar and order a whiskey.

The tall man fingered his glass, then placed it on the bar. He turned back to watch Dawson, but his gaze rested on Farley a moment.

Farley smiled and slipped down the bar to him. He leaned back, matching the tall man's posture until the man faced him.

'Howdy,' Farley said, smiling.

'Howdy to you,' the tall man said. 'This storyteller tells a good story. So good, I wonder whether to believe everything I'm hearing.'

Farley scratched his chin. 'You should believe it. As you know Wiley Douglas, you'll know he deserves everything that came to him.'

'I knew Wiley,' the tall man said. 'The meanest varmint in the West deserved to die. At least I assume that's where this story ends.'

'Sure does.'

The tall man chuckled. 'Good. What happened to the rest of Dirtwood's townsfolk? Did the ruthless Wiley kill the rest of them before he met his end? Or was he the only one to die in his villainous reign of terror?'

Farley shrugged. 'He only killed a sheriff.'

'What a strange tale! Meanest varmint in the West rides into a pathetic town like Dirtwood. He kills one person, then dies. Perhaps this tale ain't so good after all.'

'The truth ain't always as entertaining as stories.'

'Some people don't know the difference between truth and stories.'

The tall man turned and grabbed his glass. He ran a long finger around the top of the glass, then placed it down. With a short gesture, he poured a small puddle of whiskey on to the bar.

Farley nodded at the whiskey. 'You drinking that or are you just wasting it?'

'I've anticipated this drink for seven years. I'll enjoy anticipating it a while longer.' He smiled at Farley. 'You heading back to Dirtwood after you and your friend have finished entertaining this saloon with your truthful stories?'

Farley nodded. 'Sure.'

'Mind if I ride along with you and see this town?'

'Why? As we've removed Wiley, there ain't much to see.'

The tall man pushed his drink from him and stood back.

'Maybe not, but I fancy having my drink in the saloon there.'

As the tall man wasn't taking his drink, Farley grabbed the glass and knocked back the whiskey.

'You have friends in Dirtwood?'

'Used to.' The tall man smiled and patted Farley's shoulder. 'I have new friends now.'

CHAPTER 4

Ethan and Cooper reached Hail Ridge in three days. Cooper pushed his horses more than usual, reducing a four- and often five-day journey.

With its rows of rough buildings and bustling activity, Hail Ridge resembled most frontier towns – Dirtwood included before Josh arrived – and Ethan couldn't stop a smile emerging as they rode down the road.

Most people they passed waved and Cooper waved back and offered a quip or two. At the store he halted and turned to Ethan.

'End of the road for you, Ethan.'

'Yeah, but before you leave, let me buy you a drink.'

'No need. You got plenty of need for your money and I ain't got a need for a whiskey.'

Ethan extracted his few coins from his pocket.

'I got no need for a drink either, but I need to buy information. Saloon is the best place to start.'

Cooper chuckled. 'Wait here. Let someone who knows how to do this do the talking.'

Cooper jumped from the cart and slipped into the store. With nothing to do, Ethan jumped down too and watched the townsfolk bustle pass.

When Cooper emerged he nodded to the saloon.

'Your instincts were right. Man you want is in the saloon.'

'What does he look like?'

'You can't mistake him.' Cooper patted Ethan on the back. 'I'll leave the rest of the talking to you.'

Ethan tipped his hat. 'Thank you kindly.'

As Cooper wandered back into the store, Ethan strode to the saloon. Inside, a few drinkers sat around tables, but as promised, Ethan saw the man he wanted within seconds.

Leaned over the bar was an angular man. Seen in profile, his face was hard-boned. Although he hadn't moved when Ethan entered the saloon, Ethan knew that he'd sized him up.

Ethan sauntered across the saloon and leaned on the bar beside him. 'You be Blake Reynolds?' he asked with a cough.

The man stared into his glass and swirled the contents. 'You found him,' he said, his voice deep.

Ethan held out his hand. 'I'm Ethan Craig. I hail from Dirtwood and I have some work for you.'

Blake glanced at Ethan's hand, then turned back to his drink.

'Ain't looking for work so you've wasted a journey.'

In a self-conscious gesture, Ethan placed his hand behind his back and slipped closer to Blake.

'This is work you're suited to.'

Blake sipped his whiskey and licked his lips.

'It might be, but I'm resting up. So go back to your town and find someone who ain't resting up.'

'I ain't going until you hear me out.'

Blake hailed the bartender for another drink.

'You can stay and maybe if you stay long enough, I might have finished resting up. Then I'll be ready to think about it.' Blake sneered. 'But you'll have a long wait.'

Ethan nodded. 'Couldn't ask for more. Man has a right to rest. I'll explain what I got, and you can decide what to do.'

'Don't waste your breath. You can't afford my services.'

Ethan took a deep breath. 'How much?'

Blake lifted the glass to his lips, then set it down without drinking. He smiled.

'One thousand dollars.'

'You're a right funny man.' Ethan glanced away. 'Tell me what you really need.'

When Ethan turned back, Blake was still smiling.

'You heard right the first time. I need one thousand dollars. Anything less and I stay here, drinking my whiskey and enjoying the view while I rest up.'

Ethan gulped and glanced down. 'You got it then.'

Blake widened his smile into a grin. 'You ain't got one thousand dollars' worth of trouble.'

'I reckon I have.'

Blake signalled to the bartender for another glass of whiskey and pushed it to Ethan.

'You must need me mighty bad.'

Ethan wrapped his hands around the drink and leaned on the bar, letting the smell of his first whiskey in weeks water his mouth.

'I do need you mighty bad.' Ethan gulped his

41

whiskey and bared his teeth. 'The bounty will come to that.'

Blake licked his lips. 'Even for a man who's resting up, you have my attention. Who you got?'

'The Carters.'

Blake narrowed his eyes. 'I've heard of them. Farley has a quick hand but Josh's just a bully with a brighter brother to protect him. They wouldn't be worth more than a hundred dollars.'

Ethan leaned forward. 'They have a hired gun, Vince McGiven.'

'Heard of him too. Again, he ain't worth more than a hundred dollars – if that. Who else you got?'

'They have various ruffians with them, about twenty in all.'

'This ain't like shopping at the store. If I brought them all in, I doubt I'd get half-way to reaching my price.'

'Except Josh shot a lawman.'

Blake rubbed his jaw and contemplated his drink.

'Never heard about that.'

'Nobody outside of Dirtwood knows and unless you bring in the Carters, that might not get known.'

'Sounds like a tall tale to me,' Blake said. He smiled. Then the smile disappeared. 'Go tell it to someone else.'

'You're the man I've picked to tell it to. You're my last hope.'

'Hate to disappoint a man – except today.'

Ethan sipped his whiskey, forcing his anger to stay bottled.

'Have you heard of Dirtwood? It used to be a fine

town like Hail Ridge until Josh rode into town. Life ain't been fine since. We tried a—'

Blake grabbed Ethan's arm. 'Enough! Your pleading's doing nothing for me. Take my advice. When ruffians ride into town, get your townsfolk together and sort it. If that fails, get a lawman. If that fails—'

'We've tried all that. That's why I'm here talking to a low-life leech like you.'

Blake laughed. 'You know how to talk a man round to your way of thinking. But you only talk to low-life leeches like me if you have a thousand dollars' worth of trouble.'

Ethan gulped the last of his drink and slammed the glass on the bar. 'I have that much trouble.'

'Prove it, and you can consider me hired.'

'Come to Dirtwood and I will.'

'Prefer some wanted posters with those people's faces under some figures that add up to one thousand dollars.'

Ethan grabbed Blake's arm and swung him round to face him.

'I'd heard you were the best. You're worth squat.'

'I *am* the best. Hence the price.' Blake patted his gunbelt. 'Scat.'

'You won't kill me, so I'm here, standing beside you and spoiling your resting-up time until you change your mind.'

Blake removed his hand from his gunbelt and grabbed his whiskey. 'You'll have a long stay.'

'Got no reason to go.'

Blake nodded and set his glass on the bar. He glanced away, then drove his fist into Ethan's jaw.

The next Ethan knew he was sitting outside on the

boardwalk, his head spinning. People wandered by him muttering about drunkards and Cooper stood over him, shaking his head.

'So Blake ain't interested in your offer,' he said, smiling.

Ethan rubbed his chin and forced a smile. 'I wasn't persuasive enough. I need to negotiate some more.'

Cooper sighed. 'See sense, Ethan. From what I heard, Blake near busted your jaw. Next time he'll kill you. Come on. I'll head north and get you half-way home. You can find another bounty hunter. They're everywhere. We can leave a message that we're interested. Soon someone will hear—'

'If Blake can't help us, we're doomed,' Ethan shouted. He probed his jaw and jumped to his feet. 'He's here and so am I. By nightfall, he's coming with me to Dirtwood.'

'Bull-headed idiot.'

Ethan grinned. 'I know.'

Cooper chuckled. 'That wasn't a compliment.'

Ethan batted the dust from his clothes and strode into the saloon. With his shoulders shrugged high, he stormed to the bar.

Blake still stood at the bar. Without turning, he chuckled.

'Reckon you still ain't listening.'

'You reckoned right,' Ethan muttered, lifting his fists. 'But this time it's you who's listening.'

Blake put down his glass and turned. As soon as he saw Ethan's raised fists, he smiled.

'You have more guts than I expected. Put down those fists while you still can.'

'Can't do that.'

Blake shook his head. 'As I'm resting up, I ain't in the mood for killing anyone today.'

'So I'm staying here, waiting to hire you.'

Blake sighed and glanced away. Then with alarming speed, he dived at Ethan, catching him full in the chest and bundling him to the floor.

Ethan had anticipated the move and as he fell back, he rolled with the blow. Both men landed side by side. Ethan rolled on to Blake and pinned his shoulders to the floor, but Blake bucked him away. Ethan crashed into a table, scattering the people sitting around it. He leapt to his feet and hurled chairs from him.

Blake rolled to his feet too and grinned while Ethan cleared a space.

'I ain't beaten sense into anyone for a while. Thanks for the opportunity.'

'Only person having sense beaten into them is you.' Ethan spat on his hands and raised his fists. 'Only question is how much I have to beat you to make you listen.'

Moving slowly, Blake reached to his gunbelt. Ethan tensed, but Blake slipped the belt from his waist and laid it behind him on the bar. Then he glanced around the saloon.

'Anyone who comes within ten feet of my gun will die,' he shouted. Several people backed as Blake turned back to Ethan. 'But *you* are about to get the hiding of a lifetime.'

'I've had some of those recently. I'm ready to hand one out.'

Blake beckoned Ethan closer.

Ethan took a long step and feinted left and right,

both blows landing short of Blake. With his fists at waist level, Blake kept his ground.

Ethan feinted again, then on the second blow turned it into a solid slug at Blake's head. Blake hurled up his forearm blocking the blow and slugged his right fist into Ethan's guts.

At the last second, Ethan saw the blow coming and rolled with the punch. But it knocked him to the floor. He glanced up to confirm that Blake wasn't following through with another punch.

Then he rolled to his feet. Ethan lifted his fists again.

'Is that the best you can do?' he shouted.

Blake smiled, then hurled a flurry of blows at Ethan. Ethan blocked the first but the blows landed on his chest and arms battering them numb. In a desperate lunge, Ethan bundled Blake back against the bar, but Blake squirmed out and kicked his feet from under him.

With a bone-crunching thud, Ethan's chin hit the floor and he lay a moment, tasting blood. To clear his throat he spat and rolled back on to his feet. This time, slower than before.

Blake smiled. 'You've had enough.'

With a great roar, Ethan charged at Blake. He kept his head down and whirled his fists. In his berserk action, he delivered a few blows before a solid punch to the jaw sent him reeling back to fall over a table.

He lay a moment getting his breath, then sat. Someone hurled a bucket of water over him. He spat the water away, gasping.

'Thanks,' he muttered.

With his hands on his hips, Blake glared at him.

46

'Had enough?'

'Nope. Just getting my second wind.'

As Ethan staggered to his feet and tottered, Blake shook his head and lowered his fists.

'Your second wind will mount to squat.'

Ethan spat on the floor and staggered two paces. He whirled his arm, his fist thudding into Blake's stomach, although he'd been aiming for his face. His second blow bounced off Blake's chest.

'Enough,' Blake said. 'Save your strength for getting someone else to go to your god-forsaken town. Dirty Ridge is it?'

'Dirtwood,' Ethan roared. 'Don't forget it ever again.'

He slammed his fist into Blake's jaw. The blow landed with so little force that Blake just smiled and pushed Ethan back.

'Give up, Edward,' he said, turning to the bar.

'Ethan, my name's Ethan and I come from Dirtwood.' Ethan stormed to Blake. 'And don't turn your back on me.'

He pulled Blake around and swung his fist. It missed Blake by feet.

Blake shrugged and, with the flat of his hand, clubbed Ethan across the side of the head.

Blackness and motes of lights danced around Ethan as he lay stunned, until another bucket of water slapped him in the face. He still lay until a second bucket brought him back.

He glanced up. Cooper stood over him, shaking his head.

'There's a time to fight,' Cooper said, 'and there's a

time to give up. This is the time to give up.'

Ethan spat on the floor and staggered to his feet. He tottered backwards and Cooper held him up.

'Point me at him,' Ethan muttered.

'I'll point you to the door and fresh air.'

Ethan pushed Cooper away. He orientated himself and aimed at the bar. He staggered to within three paces of Blake and stood with his hands on his hips, swaying back and forth.

'You can knock me down,' he shouted. 'You can knock me down again. You can kill me. But I ain't going anywhere until you go to Dirtwood.'

Blake sipped his whiskey. He turned and considered his half-empty glass. He shrugged.

'Can I finish my whiskey first?'

CHAPTER 5

In late morning, riding on the horse he'd borrowed from Cooper, Ethan approached the few ramshackle buildings that were the extent of Dirtwood. Blake Reynolds rode alongside, his back straight and his gaze set forward.

Ethan coughed and glanced to his side. 'You ain't asked for details of what we're facing.'

'Don't need to,' Blake said. 'I know the type.'

'That's what Sheriff Ogden said and they killed him.'

'I ain't Sheriff Ogden. I follow my own rules.' Blake turned to Ethan and frowned. 'You'd better hope these people amount to one thousand dollars.'

Ethan gulped. 'And if they don't?'

'You'll pay the difference.'

Ethan stared at Blake, judging if he was serious, but his craggy features were as inscrutable as ever.

As they rode into Dirtwood, Blake stared at each building that they passed. At the saloon, he alighted. As he tethered his horse, Ethan jumped down and glanced through the dusty saloon window.

Inside, three of Josh's men sat around a table playing

poker. Ethan relayed this information to Blake, who shrugged and strode into the saloon and straight to the bar. Ethan followed.

Rock glared at Ethan and snarled.

'We told you, Ethan. You ain't welcome here, not unless you're volunteering to give Josh whipping practice.'

'Go to hell, Rock.'

Rock snarled and glanced towards the bar.

'Same goes for your new friend. Any friend of yours ain't welcome here – unless he wants his hide ripped to shreds.'

Blake turned and leaned on the bar. 'Is that how you greet strangers in Dirtwood?'

Rock shrugged. 'Only the ones we don't know.'

The other men chuckled as Rock laughed at his wit.

Blake glanced at the brown stain in the middle of the saloon and pushed from the bar.

'As you don't know me, I suppose I'd better go.'

Rock turned back to his poker-game and the other men leaned over the table.

Blake pulled his gun and blasted lead through the nearest poker-players' backs. As they fell, a third shot rang out, wheeling Rock's gun from his hand as he dragged it from its holster.

In three long paces Blake stormed across the saloon. He grabbed Rock's collar and hoisted him close to his face.

'Just so we ain't strangers, the name's Blake Reynolds. Can you remember that?'

Rock nodded, his shoulders shaking in Blake's hand.

'I will.'

'Good. Go explain to Josh that I'm here.'

'I'll do that,' Rock whined, his eyes rolling.

Blake hurled him to the floor and with a round-footed kick, pushed him to the saloon doors.

Rock rolled to a stop. He glared back, then scampered through the swing-doors and across the road.

Blake strode to the bar. He leaned against it and stared at the two bodies.

'I'm nowhere near my thousand dollars yet. Those two weren't worth the price of a bullet.'

Ethan sighed and peered through the window.

'In the next few minutes you'll be closer to that price.'

Ethan edged to one of the bodies. With the toe of his boot, he kicked it over, then slipped off the man's gunbelt. He shuffled it around his waist and pulled the holster round to rest on his hip. He shrugged the belt to a comfortable height and pulled the gun twice, familiarizing himself with the weapon.

'Leave this to me,' Blake muttered, watching Ethan with a wry smile. 'This ain't a fist-fight, where you get some bruises for your trouble.'

'I know what to do. Never killed a man before, but I'm defending my town and I—'

'Spare me the heroic speech. I don't care about your two-bit town, just what I can get for Josh's and Farley's hides.'

Ethan nodded. 'I know. You can fight for dollars, but let me fight for what I believe in.'

As Blake sneered, Ethan glanced through the window.

Josh and Rock strode across the road with Vince

behind them. Josh stopped in the centre of the road and folded his arms.

'Rock says you shot two of my men,' Josh shouted.

Ethan glanced at Blake who leaned against the bar, cleaning imaginary dust off his gun barrel.

Ethan cleared his throat. 'You're right, Josh. Two bodies are littering up the saloon.'

'Ethan, you've irritated me once too often. Send out Blake. When we've dealt with him, what we did to Wiley will seem like Christmas Day compared to what you'll get.'

Ethan glanced at Blake, who holstered his gun.

'Blake ain't coming out. If you want to talk to him, you'll have to come in.'

Josh gestured to Vince. They shared low words. Then Vince sauntered across the road and clattered on to the boardwalk.

With his arms straight, Vince pushed open the swing-doors and strode inside. He held on to the doors and glanced at the bodies, then at Blake. Sneering, he turned to Ethan.

'Who's your new quiet friend?'

Ethan shrugged. 'Guessing Rock didn't relay the information we told him to or you ain't bright enough to understand. This man is Blake Reynolds.'

'I know,' Vince spat. 'I mean who is he, thinking he can come into our town and shoot up law-abiding folk?'

'Blake is the best bounty hunter around.'

With a contemptuous lunge, Vince pushed through the doors and let them squeak to a halt behind him.

'How come I never heard of him?'

Blake chuckled. Moving slowly, he swung round and

leaned back so his elbows rested on the bar.

'Pour three drinks, bartender,' he muttered.

With his hand shaking, Doc clattered three glasses on the bar and filled them with whiskey.

Using the tips of his forefinger and thumb, Blake took the first glass and sauntered along the bar. He placed the glass before Vince and sauntered back. Then he placed the second drink in the centre of the bar. Only then did he sip the third drink.

Vince nodded. 'Much obliged for the drink.' He sauntered to the bar and took the whiskey.

Ethan glanced between the two men, then strode to the bar.

'Stop, Ethan,' Blake said without turning. 'That ain't your drink.'

Ethan shrugged. 'Whose drink is it?'

Blake lifted his glass to his lips.

'This is my drink. Vince has his own drink. The third is for whichever one of us is still alive in two minutes.'

Vince chuckled and gulped his whiskey in one swallow.

Blake sipped his whiskey, his eyes only for the rows of bottles behind the bar.

'Did you enjoy your last drink?' he muttered. 'Even scum like you deserve a drink before they die.'

Vince contemplated his empty glass, then screeched it back along the bar.

'I'm ready for a second drink.'

Blake nodded and gulped the remains of his whiskey.

'You're eager to die. I can't blame you. Living in that smelly hide can't be fun.'

Vince smiled and, moving his body with extreme

slowness, swung into the centre of the saloon.

'Time for talking is at an end, bounty hunter. Let's get to it.'

Blake nodded and stood before Vince. He set his legs wide and smiled.

'How much does Josh pay you?'

Vince hunched forward. 'Quit talking.'

'I was just totting up how much you might fetch.' Blake frowned. 'Guess it ain't much. Maybe I'll get ten dollars for your gun and five dollars for your clothes. The hide inside is worth squat.'

'You talk too much.'

'Then quit listening and get to it, little man.'

Vince smiled. 'Good try. Guess you need to rile me so that you can take me.'

Vince glanced to the side. Then he whirled his hand. Two gunshots blasted, sounding as one as they echoed through the saloon.

Ethan pulled his own gun, but stopped himself from firing as Vince staggered back a pace. A reddening flood spread across his shirt. Then Vince fell to his knees and on to his front.

Blake sauntered to the body, his gun arm held down. He pulled his shirt round to consider a rip along the sleeve.

'Came close. I'll give him that.'

He pushed Vince's head to one side, then kicked him over. The surge of blood flooding from under the body made Ethan wince.

Ethan dashed to the window. Outside, the rest of Josh's men had grouped in the centre of the road.

'They're wondering what's happened,' Ethan said.

54

Blake grabbed the glass in the centre of the bar.

'Yeah, but if I were you, I'd worry about what'll happen now.'

'And what *will* happen?'

Blake knocked back the whiskey and wiped his hand across his mouth. He sighed.

'It can go two ways. If they have sense, they'll storm the saloon. We'll take some of them before they kill us, but we won't stand a chance.'

Ethan gulped. 'And the other way?'

'They'll preserve their worthless hides and hang back to see what we do. They'll send some at us, but the rest will run.'

'I hope they ain't got sense then.'

Blake chuckled. 'Don't doubt it. Outlaws lack the sense they were born with. That's why I do what I do. It's time to give them a nudge in the right direction.'

'Can I help?'

Blake sauntered to the swing-doors.

'Sure. Get ready to fire when I give the word.'

Ethan flexed his gun-hand and joined Blake by the door.

Outside, Josh wandered two paces closer.

'You all right, Vince?' he shouted.

Blake laughed. 'Vince ain't coming out. He's too busy bleeding all over the floor.'

With an angry slam of his fist against his thigh, Josh grunted orders to his men that Ethan couldn't hear. His men fanned out across the road.

Blake swung into the doorway and fired a rapid series of shots. Ethan jumped to the side. He smashed a window and fired through it at the two nearest men. Returning

55

gunfire exploded around him, spraying him with glass shards and, with no choice, he leapt to the floor.

He glanced up. Blake stood with his back to the wall by the swing-doors. When a lull in the gunfire came, Blake swung back to the door and fired twice more, spinning back to hide afterwards.

When the next burst of gunfire ended, Ethan glanced over the windowsill. Outside, two bodies lay on the ground and the rest of Josh's men were hightailing it back across the road.

'We've seen them off,' Ethan shouted.

Blake strode to Vince's body and removed his gun. With the two guns held before him, he shrugged.

'We ain't seen them off.' Blake smiled. 'That comes now.'

Blake took a deep breath, then charged through the swing-doors, his two guns blasting in all directions.

'What happened then?' Felix asked.

Ethan took a deep breath and glanced around his barn. Felix, Herb and Peter leaned forward and grinned. Ethan licked his lips.

'Blake charged from the saloon. He had a gun in each hand and he fired and fired. The few of Josh's men who hadn't run stood a moment. Then they panicked. One leapt through Peter's window.' Ethan glanced at Peter. 'Sorry your store got messed up.'

Peter shrugged. 'Don't matter. Carry on with the tale.'

'Josh backtracked the fastest. He dashed straight to the stable, leapt on his horse, and rode out of town like the devil himself was on his tail.'

'Sounds like he was,' Felix said.

Everyone chuckled.

'Afterwards none of the ruffians hung around. Some went north, some went south, and the rest didn't go anywhere.'

Herb sighed. 'Did you take any, Ethan?'

'Don't reckon so. I fired at some, but I ain't like Blake. He killed six men and if they hadn't hightailed it out of here, he'd have killed the other fourteen, make no mistake.'

Everyone patted each other on the back and offered a round of agreement.

Felix lifted a hand for quiet. 'Hate to say this, Ethan, but Dirtwood has rules. You must promise you won't ignore us again. You could have got us killed and don't say that you didn't, because that ain't the point.'

Ethan nodded. 'You're right, but I'm glad we're alive to debate that point.'

'I'll leave it at that, but it still leaves two questions.' Felix lifted two fingers. 'First, will Josh return?'

'And what about Farley?' Herb asked. 'He didn't strike me as someone who'd worry about facing Blake.'

Ethan smiled. 'Blake doesn't worry about facing anyone. He took Vince. So the likes of Farley won't concern him.'

Herb leaned forward. 'But he's staying to defend us, ain't he?'

'Blake doesn't care about justice, our problems, or protecting us. He only cares about collecting his bounty. But I guess he thinks that the Carters will return. If he thought otherwise, he'd be after them. So he's protecting us, but only indirectly.'

Felix snorted. 'Much as I figured and why I thought this was dangerous.'

Ethan tried to stop himself sneering. He couldn't.

'You only hate that I didn't do what you told me to do,' he spat. 'You ain't in charge.'

'I ain't. But then again, neither are you.'

'But why can't you admit that I did the right thing?'

With his eyes downcast, Felix shrugged.

'Because you didn't.'

'And?' Ethan whispered.

Felix sighed and looked at Ethan.

'And I'm glad your plan worked, but calling in a bounty hunter has raised the stakes and we have to hope that it don't backfire on us.'

'Blake will see them off.'

'That ain't my concern.' Felix lifted his hand, showing two fingers outstretched, and bent one finger down. 'My second question worries me the most. What happens if the Carters don't return?'

Ethan raised his eyebrows and everyone shrugged.

'Don't get you.'

'Like I thought, Ethan,' Felix shouted, waving his hands above his head. 'You charged off to Hail Ridge without thinking about the consequences. You fetched the roughest bounty hunter you could find – a man who doesn't get his gun out of its holster for less than one thousand dollars. He won't get that sort of money for Vince. So what will he do if the Carters don't return? We can't raise the difference.'

Ethan gulped. 'How much could we raise between us?'

Felix looked around the group. 'I have some hidden and I guess so has everyone else. If it amounts to one hundred dollars between us, I'll be surprised. That won't satisfy Blake. Then we could find ourselves in an even worse mess.'

'Then I'll talk to him.'

Felix shrugged. 'You will.'

CHAPTER 6

For the next three mornings, Blake rose from Ethan's barn and rode into Dirtwood. He went straight to the saloon, leaned on the bar, and consumed a bottle of whiskey at a steady rate. From time to time, the towns-folk looked in. Some even returned to the saloon for the first time since the troubles began, but nobody approached him.

When night fell, Blake rode back to Ethan's house, where Martha fed him his meal. He ate, saying nothing, then with the barest nod of appreciation, sauntered to the barn for the night.

Each day, Ethan avoided facing his problem. He also avoided Martha's accusing gaze and returned to his farm duties, losing himself in the activities that had previously filled his life.

But on the fourth morning, as Blake rode down the trail into Dirtwood, Ethan threw down his shovel and strode to the edge of his field.

' 'Morning, Blake,' he hollered.

Blake halted. He glanced at the fields and sighed.

' 'Morning to you too.'

'I've spoken to everyone. We're happy you're around and you're welcome to stay as long as you like.' Ethan took a deep breath. 'But we wanted to know how long that might be.'

Blake stared along the trail to Dirtwood.

'Depends on Josh.'

Ethan sighed. 'We thought as much. Will he return?'

'Can go two ways.'

'It can, but you don't intend to go after him?'

'Nope. Not when I'm resting up. No use getting all riled tracking Josh over half the state. I've thrown down my challenge. Got to wait for him to take up on it.'

Ethan took a deep breath. 'What happens if he don't take the bait?'

Blake shrugged. 'He lives.'

'And you don't get your thousand dollars.'

Blake leaned forward in the saddle and smiled.

'Excepting you promised me one thousand dollars if I came to Dirtwood.'

'I did.' Ethan gulped. 'We've talked about what we can raise if Josh don't return. We're a poor town, but we pull together when we're in trouble. You'll get something for Vince's hide and then . . .'

Blake breathed in the cool morning air.

'Winter's a-coming and travelling men like me find life on the trail hard in those months. I'd planned to rest up in Hail Ridge until you gave my fists some work. Dirtwood is as nice as you said it was. A man could enjoy resting up here through the winter.'

Ethan sighed and tipped his hat. 'And the townsfolk will be pleased to have your company this winter. For as long as you want, you have lodgings, whiskey, and if there's anything else, just say.'

'I have simple needs. You've mentioned them all.'

'And after that?'

'Come spring, I'll search for one thousand dollars' worth of trouble.'

Blake swung his horse away and trotted towards Dirtwood.

Ethan couldn't stop a grin breaking out. He punched the air and whistled a merry tune. When his first flush of excitement ended, he glanced up.

From across the fields, Herb ran towards him.

With a huge smile on his lips, Ethan trotted across the fields to Herb.

'Great news,' he hollered when he was a dozen yards from his friend. 'Blake is staying all winter. We have protection and he ain't riled at us and . . .'

Ethan hung his head, trailing off his good news as he saw Herb's wide-eyed glare.

Herb placed his hands on his knees, gulping in long racking breaths.

'He's . . . They're . . . We got . . .' he said between gasps.

'Slow down,' Ethan said, patting Herb on the back and pulling him up straight. 'Guess that Josh has returned. Is Farley with him?'

Herb opened his mouth, but only mumbled words emerged.

Ethan turned back to the trail.

'Blake, Blake Reynolds,' he hollered. 'You'd better come here. Herb has news.'

Blake turned his horse. He clumped back down the trail and across the fields towards them.

'Got terrible news,' Herb muttered, when his reddened face was less glowing.

'I guessed,' Ethan said. 'Save it till Blake's here.'

Herb nodded and gasped another long breath.

Blake swung off his horse and strode to them.

'Guess Josh has returned with Farley,' he said. 'That's their last mistake.'

Herb nodded. 'They have, but that ain't the worst of it.'

Blake shrugged. 'How many are with them?'

'It ain't how many. It's who's with them.' Herb turned to Ethan. 'I'm sorry, but Luke McCoy is riding with them.'

Ethan hung his head and gulped. 'Then this is the end.'

'Who in tarnation is Luke McCoy?' Blake asked.

Ethan stared straight ahead, directing his cart towards Dirtwood. At his side, Herb also looked straight ahead. So far, Ethan hadn't trusted himself to speak.

Only when the row of buildings on the outskirts of Dirtwood approached did the realization of what he was facing return. He straightened and turned to Herb.

'Get word to everyone. This is a town matter. Everyone needs to get to Dirtwood.'

Herb nodded and took a deep breath. He jumped from the cart and ran back along the trail. Then he veered into the fields heading for the nearest farm – Felix's.

They rode in silence before Ethan turned to Blake.

'Luke McCoy used to live in Dirtwood. He and I were friends, but seven years ago we quarrelled over my ex-wife, Judith . . .' Ethan sighed. 'She never spoke about what Luke meant to her, but that didn't matter after Luke shot Caleb Dalton, Judith's pa.'

Blake sighed. 'Luke sounds like plenty of bad.'

'He is. Felix, Herb and Peter overpowered Luke and held him in the saloon. Then everyone voted. I said we should string him up, but the decision came down to getting in the law. Marshal Devine came and took Luke away. We learnt later that he was rotting in Beaver Ridge jail.'

'Except he's back.' Blake rubbed his chin. 'How tough does he think he is?'

'He was a high-spirited youngster, but I always thought he'd be an asset to Dirtwood – life here is hard enough without finding time for troublemaking. But he ain't returned to settle down and raise a family.'

Blake nodded. 'Guess an escaped prisoner will be worth something.'

Ethan shrugged. 'Guess he would.'

They rode to the outskirts of Dirtwood and pulled up. The road was deserted, but someone had strung up a row of horses outside the saloon and the stable doors down the road were wide open.

Blake sighed. 'From what you've said, you have unfinished business with Luke. You have the right to decide that business with him.'

'Stopped hating Luke long ago. Don't matter to me what happens to him. If he's returned for trouble, he deserves to die. I have no compunction about shooting him but if the bullet ain't mine, I ain't losing sleep.'

'Understood.' Blake nodded and rubbed his chin.

'Luke McCoy – would he be blond and tall?'

'Yup.' Ethan narrowed his eyes. 'How do you know him? Until we put him away, he lived all his life in Dirtwood.'

'Didn't recall the name at first, but five years ago, he escaped from prison. He's a devious runt. It took six of us to track him.'

'So he knows you too?'

'Doubt it. I wasn't there when they found him.' Blake flexed his hand. 'He's handy with his gun too. He took two men before they got him. Pity they wasted their time taking him back to jail.'

Ethan nodded and hunched in his seat.

Thirty minutes passed before Felix drove the first cart along the trail – Herb sat alongside him.

Blake snorted. 'This don't look like much support.'

'I guess the others will follow.'

Ethan jumped from his cart and stood on the trail.

When Herb arrived, he jumped down and ruffled his thinning hair.

'Sorry about this, Ethan,' he said.

'Sorry about what?' Ethan glanced down the trail. 'When are the others coming?'

'They ain't,' Felix said, his voice low.

'You mean that just you and Herb are coming?'

Felix sighed. 'We ain't coming either. I'm here to explain what we've decided. Getting hotheaded ain't getting us out of this. We're staying out of Dirtwood, tending our animals, and bringing in the harvest.'

'And you think Luke's teaming up with Josh means he'll accept that?'

Felix sighed and set his hands on his hips.

'Luke's served his time. Getting him riled won't help. We—'

'I've heard enough,' Ethan spat. 'You're wrong. We have to face up to Josh and Luke. We have Blake Reynolds, the finest bounty hunter in the state on our side, and if we join forces, we'll outnumber them. We *will* prevail.'

'We think that not riling them is more sensible. Come back to your farm with me, Ethan.'

Felix held out a hand to shepherd Ethan to his cart, but Ethan shrugged away.

'I ain't going.' With an angry swirl of his head, he turned to Blake. 'Can you talk sense into my fellow townsfolk?'

'Nope,' Blake said with a shrug. 'Guess it's just the two of us then.'

Ethan shook his head. 'I got you into this. But if we ain't backing you, we ain't worth saving.'

'Don't care about that.' Blake drew a long breath through his teeth and glanced into Dirtwood. 'This is a calculated gamble. The price Luke will fetch is worth it – whatever the risk. I have a plan. It can still work with the two of us, if you're with me.'

Ethan glanced at Felix and Herb who jumped on their cart and swung it away from Dirtwood.

Ethan spat on the ground.

'I'm with you,' he muttered.

CHAPTER 7

In mid-afternoon, Ethan strode down Dirtwood's main road. He stood before the saloon and squared off to the doors. He cleared his throat and took a deep breath.

'Josh,' he hollered. 'You and I need to talk.'

A face appeared at the window, then ducked. Then Josh strode on to the boardwalk.

'You appear to be alone, farmer boy.' Josh tipped back his hat. 'But you calling in a bounty hunter don't seem like talking to me.'

'Thought that might be the only language you'd understand. But that ain't worked.'

Josh shrugged. Then to a nod, Luke strode on to the boardwalk. His tall, blond-haired form was unmistakable to Ethan even after seven years.

Ethan sneered, his hand drifting to his gunbelt.

'Morning, Ethan,' Luke said with his feet set wide. 'Bet you never thought you'd see me again.'

'Nope,' Ethan said and spat on the ground.

'If you're talking, Ethan, you can talk to me.'

Ethan took a deep breath. 'Why did you return?'

'If I told you, you wouldn't believe me.'

'We put you away for what you did to Caleb Dalton. I guess you ain't served your time, but you've served enough to satisfy me, and as Felix Simmons calls the shots around here, it'll satisfy everyone else.'

'Felix,' Luke muttered, bunching his hands into fists.

'You've no reason to like him, but if you don't want trouble, we won't give you any.'

'That's neighbourly of you, but I ain't satisfied with what happened to me. Seven years is a long time to think.'

'And what have you thought?'

Luke tipped back his hat and walked in a circle. When he faced Ethan, he slammed his hands on his hips.

'Seven years is a long time without whiskey. I want a drink in this saloon. When Dirtwood put me away, I'd a taste for it and through those years in prison, I wished that I could be in here supping a glass of gut-rotting brew.'

'You've done that. So you can move on.'

Luke shrugged. 'I ain't had that drink yet. Strange; when you anticipate something for years, and you get the chance, you don't fancy doing it. Perhaps I'll have it when I've finished my other business.'

Ethan gulped. 'We don't want trouble, Luke. I've forgiven you for what you did to Judith—'

'Don't go there,' Luke spat. He swirled on his heel and stormed back into the saloon, pushing the swing-doors so they crashed against the wall and creaked back and forth.

Josh grinned. 'You don't know when to shut up, Ethan. From what I've heard, getting Luke riled is the worst mistake that any man can make.'

'I knew that.'

Josh stared along the road, nodding. 'Where's your bounty hunter?'

Ethan glanced down the road at the prairies beyond. 'Worthless varmint took off.'

'And I'm supposed to believe that, am I?'

Ethan shrugged. 'Don't care what you believe.'

'You *should* care. I had to whip Wiley's hide off him before I reached the truth. Can do the same to you if I don't believe you. So what happened to the bounty hunter?'

'He saw what he faced and hightailed it out of here.' Ethan smiled with an exaggerated grin. 'His type are as low as the men they chase.'

Josh edged to the end of the boardwalk and gazed along the windows of the buildings opposite.

'So he ain't laying a trap for us?'

'That man's a coward. *You* didn't worry him though. He heard Luke was here and left with barely a word.'

Josh scratched his chin. Then he gestured into the saloon. Luke and Farley sauntered outside. They shared low words. Then Josh turned to Ethan.

'Give me the full story.'

'Herb told Blake that Luke was back and he leapt on his horse. I tried to stop him but he wouldn't listen to reason. Said he didn't care what you lowlifes did to us. It wasn't worth the risk.'

'That ain't the truth.' Josh rubbed his hands. 'I'll enjoy whipping the rest out of you.'

'Wait!' Luke shouted, grabbing Josh's arm. 'I know Ethan. I know when he's telling the truth.'

Josh raised his eyebrows. 'And is that the truth?'

'Nope, but he has one chance to tell it, then you can have him.'

Ethan hung his head and took a deep breath. When he looked up, he set his hands on his hips.

'Blake said he remembered Luke from five years back. He was part of a posse that tracked him when he escaped.'

Luke nodded. 'Ethan's telling the truth. I escaped five years ago. A posse tracked me down. That bounty hunter could have been one of them.'

'So has Blake taken off?' Josh asked.

'Yup, but he ain't taken off all scared. His type doesn't scare easily. He's fetching reinforcements. He'll probably reform his old posse. I'm worth a good price.'

Josh backed a long step. 'Told Farley you were too much trouble. This ain't our problem.'

'It ain't, but you're too late. You're associated with me. If you're here when Blake returns—'

With an oath, Josh swirled round to Ethan.

'Which way did he go?'

Ethan shrugged. 'East, I reckon – probably to Hail Ridge.'

Josh shouted orders back into the saloon and the remainder of his men charged out. To his directions they dashed across the road to the stables.

With nobody watching him, Ethan backed across the road to Peter's store. From the corner of his eye, he searched for the glint of Blake's rifle, while maintaining his downtrodden farmer act.

As Josh's men strung out across the road, a rifle shot rang out, a second following a few seconds later. One

70

man folded to the ground, followed by a second. The remaining men skidded to a halt and swirled round, searching for the location of the shooter.

Fanning a spray of bullets sideways, Ethan dashed to cover. All his shots were wild, but the extra fire forced Josh's men to dash back and forth, searching for Blake's hiding-place.

Ethan hit the ground and rolled behind a row of barrels outside Peter's store. He edged his head over the top of a barrel.

Down the road Josh's men had grouped behind a cart and fired at the stable. In the centre of the road two men lay sprawled and still.

Without a clear shot available at the cart, Ethan slipped more bullets into his gun. A hand slammed on his shoulder.

Ethan swirled round, then sighed.

'Don't do that to me, Blake,' he muttered.

Blake hunkered down beside Ethan. 'You did a good job back there. You can be convincing when you want to be.'

'Thanks. Hoped you'd take more with your first strike.'

'Yeah. They worked out I was in the stable too fast. They're brighter now they have Farley and Luke.' He nodded to the saloon. 'We're going for the saloon. We need proper cover.'

Ethan glanced at the cart where the men had ducked from view.

'We'll never cross the road. Why not try the store? It's closer.'

'Too cramped – and too little whiskey. Keep your

head low and run like you've never run before.'

'When are we going?'

'Now would be a good time.'

Blake dashed from the barrel. He swung his rifle to his shoulder and fired at the cart. Then with his head down, he hurtled across the road.

Ethan pounded after Blake, his feet sending up vast plumes of dirt as he blasted across the road. He'd reached half way before the first shot hurtled by him. Then gunfire exploded around him.

With his head low, Ethan dashed across the last half of the road faster than he thought he could ever move, gaining on Blake with each pace.

Blake leapt through the swing-doors, throwing his hands up in his dive into the saloon.

Three yards from the boardwalk, Ethan threw himself forward. He landed flat on his belly and slid beneath the swing-doors, just as a splintering blast of sustained gunfire peppered the wall and doors.

With his body tingling, he lay a moment wondering where they'd hit him. On finding he was whole he rolled to his feet and grinned madly.

Blake knelt beside the broken saloon window. As a burst of gunfire showered the glass around him, he scratched his chin.

'The store probably was a better place to make a stand,' he said. 'Fancy heading back across the road?'

'You what?' Ethan shouted, but Blake grinned at him. Ethan laughed. 'You go first. I'll follow.'

Blake chuckled. When the burst of gunfire stopped, he stared from the window. With his hand steady, he sighted down his rifle, but then put it down.

'Our position's tricky. Before, we took some and the rest ran like the cowards they are. With their cleverer newcomers, it won't be as easy. They've taken better cover and they ain't easy targets.'

'Your last plan got us this far. I'm still with you.'

'Good.' Blake flexed his hands. 'Our only chance is to take Luke. Then, most of the good ideas in this gang go with him.'

'How will you get him?'

'The simplest way. I'll offer him a drink.' Blake slipped from under the window and edged to the doors. 'Except, if I understand Josh, he won't get near that drink.'

With his eyes narrowed, Ethan smiled. 'What you planning?'

Blake tipped back his hat and raised his eyebrows. He edged as close to the swing-doors as possible without being seen from outside.

'Josh,' he shouted. 'I'm a bounty hunter. I don't care two bits what happens to Dirtwood. You can have it. I only wanted you because of what I could earn for your hide.'

'I know,' Josh shouted. 'But you should have done what we thought you'd done and headed out of here. Now you're never leaving.'

'I can still leave with your help.'

With his head down, Josh laughed. 'You're a funny man, bounty hunter. Only help we're sharing is from you providing my men with target practice.'

'Josh, I go for the biggest bounty. You ain't worth crossing the road for, but Luke's price will be around a thousand dollars. I came for you, but he's the only one

I want now. If you let me have him, I'll head out of here and you can return to what you were doing.'

Ethan sidled to Blake's side. 'You reckon when they realize that Luke's worth plenty they'll turn on him?'

'Yup,' Blake whispered. 'At the chance of a reward, pardners, brothers, pretty much anyone can turn on anyone. In the next few seconds they could kill Luke and head out of here to collect the reward.'

Ethan grinned but then shook his head. 'If that happens, you won't get your thousand dollars.'

'I said they'd head out of here looking to collect on Luke. Don't mean they'll live long enough to get it.'

A full minute passed before Josh stood from behind the cart.

'Sounds a good offer. We'll give you a chance. Come into the road and you and Luke can decide if you're collecting.'

Blake frowned. 'Of course, occasionally these people show loyalty.'

Ethan sighed. 'Perhaps you should explain the situation more.'

'Won't work. They're only showing loyalty because they're more scared of Luke than they are of me.' Blake raised his voice. 'I ain't interested, Josh. If Luke wants to face me, he'll have to come in here.'

Ethan glanced around the side of the door. Luke rose from behind the cart. Then he sauntered across the road.

'He's taking you up on the challenge,' Ethan said. 'What do you want me to do?'

Blake strolled to the bar. 'Stay out of our way.'

'You doing this fairly?'

'Yeah. Sometimes you just have to find out.'

Doc edged from his back room and with his hand shaking poured three whiskeys.

With no choice, Ethan backed from the swing-doors and sat at a table.

With his gait steady, Luke clattered on to the board-walk and strode inside. He glanced at Ethan and nodded, a wide grin breaking out.

Blake lined up his three glasses of whiskey and saun-tered down the bar. He left one glass at the far end. He sauntered back, took the second glass, and left it half-way down the bar.

Luke strode across the saloon and stared at his whiskey.

'So, Blake, you were in the posse that tracked me five years ago?'

'Yup,' Blake said, tipping back his hat. 'And you ain't half as clever as you think you are. The men that got you said you were the worst challenge they'd had. It was embarrassing to take the money for you.'

Luke shrugged. 'You're right. I was younger then. I don't make the same mistakes now.'

Blake took a long sip of his whiskey. 'You're here. That's a mistake. Proves you ain't learnt a thing.'

Luke pushed his whiskey-glass in a circle, then spun round to appraise Ethan.

'You joining us? Told you I'd anticipated having a drink in this saloon. Perhaps if you join us, I'll stop anticipating it.'

Ethan stretched his legs beside the table. 'That drink ain't mine. It's Blake's way. You and he share a last whiskey. Whoever lives has the celebratory drink.'

75

Luke glanced at the other glass. 'I'll have these two drinks later.'

Blake chuckled as he sipped his whiskey. 'Like the way you people always say that. Lost count of the number of times you've been wrong.'

'There's a first time for *you* to be wrong.'

'This ain't that time.' Blake turned from the bar and looked Luke up and down. He smiled. 'Except this ain't the first time for you.'

Luke narrowed his eyes. 'What you mean?'

'Perhaps killing you might not be in my best interest.'

Luke tapped his chin. 'You're a wise man. What're you offering?'

'I've never collected on the same man twice. Didn't amount to much last time, but this time it'll be more. If I keep you alive, a devious runt like you will probably escape one day and I can track you down again. You could keep me in work for years.'

'You ain't as wise as I thought.' Luke poured half of his whiskey on to the bar and ran his finger through the pool. 'I had my last whiskey in this saloon. I drank half a glass and put it down. Then I killed Caleb Dalton. I never finished that drink and I've been anticipating finishing it ever since. I might have it after I've killed in Dirtwood again.'

As Blake shrugged and sipped his whiskey, Ethan spat on the floor.

'Why have you returned, Luke?' Ethan shouted. 'Revenge ain't the way. I knew you before you killed Caleb. You weren't like those men out there.'

Luke glared over his shoulder. 'I wasn't. Prison changed me.'

76

'You don't have to stay that way. Judith always said you could do great things if you stayed out of trouble.'

'Judith knew me well.' Luke smiled. 'Hope you've done right by her and made her a fine husband.'

Ethan sighed and rubbed his forehead. He hung his head.

'I did,' he whispered.

'Did?'

Ethan took a deep breath, then looked at Luke.

'Judith died three years back.'

Luke paled. He gulped. He set his jaw- and cheek-muscles so hard, they seemed set to burst. With a movement that Ethan just followed, he hurled his whiskey-glass at the wall, the glass exploding into fragments.

Then Luke grabbed the bar, his breathing loud. For long moments he stood hunched.

'Let's get to it,' he whispered his voice croaking.

Blake knocked back the last of his whiskey and strode to the centre of the saloon.

Luke slouched from the bar, his hands clenched into tight fists, his eyes wide. Three paces from the bar he stopped and swung round to face Blake. He lifted to his full height and his arms slackened. The fists opened and his fingers dangled. His jaw remained firm.

'Any choice as to when we go for it?' Blake murmured.

Luke glared back at Blake. He rolled his tongue around his lips.

'Won't matter to you how we start this. Take your gun when you choose, but you won't live long enough to fire it.'

Blake nodded and stood straight.

Ethan glanced between the two men. This was only

77

the second gunfight he'd seen, but something was different. This time, Blake's stance was awkward and his shoulders twitched as he changed position.

Luke appeared to be a statue.

Ethan shifted his weight, edging his hand below the table. With Luke standing three paces before him, he wasn't in his line of vision.

The room was silent, both men radiating zones of temporary peace as they stared at each other from five paces apart.

Then Blake swung his hand to his holster. In that instant, Luke went for his gun. A single gunshot blasted.

Ethan pulled his gun, but as he swung it up, Luke had turned on his hip and had his gun trained on him. Ethan stopped with his gun just out of its holster. He stared at Luke's smoking gun.

Blake dropped to his knees. His unfired gun slipped back into its holster. He glanced up. His mouth opened to say something. Then he keeled over on to his front.

Luke didn't look back at Blake but smiled at Ethan.

'Put that gun away, Ethan,' he whispered.

Ethan slammed the gun on the table and despite the situation, he whistled under his breath.

'Where did you learn to fire like that?'

'I always had the reflexes, but prison does things to a man. Those who don't keep their wits don't live long.'

Ethan nodded and glanced outside; Josh and his men were storming across the road to the saloon.

'They're confident you'd live.'

Luke grinned at Ethan. 'They were right. And you'll wish you'd died with Blake.'

CHAPTER 8

'I wasn't one of the ones who put you away, Luke,' Ethan muttered. 'We were friends. That has to count for something.'

To free the cramps Ethan flexed his shoulders. For the last hour Josh had suspended him from the ceiling with the same rope he'd used to string up Wiley, and the pain was eroding his temper. He glanced around the saloon at the men that surrounded him.

The men stared back, their eyes wide and their smiles bright in the gathering gloom.

Luke nodded. 'Yeah. Friends will do anything for each other. Sometimes they even kill each other, especially when a woman is involved.'

'Don't go there. Judith is long gone and nothing will change that.'

With his head down, Luke paced in a circle.

'How did she die?'

Ethan gulped, forcing his mind back to those desperate days.

'Three winters ago it was fearsome cold and a lung disease came.' He glanced at Doc, who looked away.

'We ain't got much doctoring here and it took four before it stopped tormenting us. Judith was the last to die. She tended the sick when others stayed away.'

Luke stopped his pacing and faced Ethan. 'She always was too good for her own well-being.'

'You mean she was too good for you.'

'That's what I said.'

'At least we agree on something.' Ethan flexed his shoulders. 'But we used to agree on more.'

'Really? Seven years ago, you wanted to string me up.'

Ethan smiled. 'Yeah. Caleb didn't deserve to die for saying Judith was too good for you. I'd have ripped you in shreds and fed you to the buzzards if I could.'

'You're the only honest person in this worthless town. Only question is – is that honesty enough to let you live?'

'Your choice, Luke. If you let me live, I'll kill you.'

'That boast ain't your way.'

As Ethan hung his head, Luke sauntered back across the saloon.

Josh ran the bullwhip through his fingers.

'You finished talking to your friend?'

'Suppose so,' Luke said.

Josh grinned. 'If you hate this man as much as I do, you can take the first swipes. I'll take over when your arm tires. After I've finished whatever's left won't be big enough to entice the buzzards.'

Luke held out his hand and Josh slammed the bullwhip handle into it. He splayed out the whip and flexed his arm.

Although he tried not to, Ethan tensed.

'Cut him down!' someone shouted.

Luke spun from Ethan. He held his hands wide.

'Can you fire that rifle?'

Sam stepped into the saloon and gestured with his rifle.

'I've shot for food and I've shot to remove vermin,' he muttered. 'I can do the latter tonight.'

'One man with a rifle ain't worrying us.'

'Maybe not, but I ain't alone.' Sam stood aside and Peter and Morgan stepped into the saloon light. Behind them others, including Felix and Herb, edged forward.

Luke nodded. He glanced at Josh, who sauntered to the rope holding Ethan. With his knife Josh severed the rope with a single swipe.

Ethan tumbled to the floor and lay a moment, enjoying feeling his muscles relax. He rolled to his knees and flexed his arms. Then he rolled back on to his haunches and stood. Placing each foot behind him with deliberate slowness, he backed to stand alongside Sam.

'Sure am glad to see you,' he whispered.

With his rifle Sam gestured into the saloon.

'You people stand back and there will be no more trouble.'

Josh grinned and swaggered to the back wall with his men. Each man looped his thumbs into his gunbelt and smiled at Sam.

Sam backed to the door and paced outside to join the other townsfolk. As Sam swung the rifle on to his shoulder, Ethan joined them.

Herb and a few townsfolk patted Sam on the back.

Then they grouped together and backed across the road.

'Don't go,' Ethan snapped. 'We have to run them out of town.'

Felix shook his head. 'We ain't here for trouble. Sam did what he came to do. I still ain't approving of what you and Blake attempted, but Sam's saved your hide and the matter's closed. We've imposed order, and things can settle down.'

As Felix turned, Ethan grabbed his shoulder and swung him back.

'We have no order. We run them out of town. Then we can have order.'

'You don't understand, Ethan,' Felix murmured, his voice tired beyond his years. 'Descending to Josh's level does no good.'

Ethan set his hands on his hips and stared at the receding townsfolk.

'So are you just walking away and returning to your farming? You just hoping Josh and Luke will get bored with hanging around the saloon and go somewhere else?'

Felix smiled. 'There's hope for you, Ethan. You've understood the plan that we agreed to follow.'

Ethan walked in a circle. He stopped and faced the few remaining townsfolk, who backed and glanced amongst each other.

'You don't get it, do you?' he shouted. 'This is our only chance to sort this. We're together. We have them worried or they'd have retaliated. We storm in there and give them the ultimatum – they leave Dirtwood or we kill them. Once they know we're together, they'll never return. If we walk away, they'll take us down one at a time.'

Within a few seconds, Ethan was talking to himself. Everyone disappeared into the dark. The trundling sounds of cartwheels receded into the distance, leaving Ethan standing alone before the saloon.

With a shiver, he glanced at the rectangle of light shining through the saloon doorway. Chuckles and contented chatter drifted outside.

Ethan gritted his teeth. Then, with an angry kick at the soil, he stormed down the road to his cart.

As he swung the cart past the saloon, Luke's laughter echoed in the night.

Ethan expected trouble to follow. He spent the night perched in his barn, his rifle loaded as he watched the trail to his farm.

But the night passed peacefully, as did the following three days.

Bit by bit, Ethan forced himself to return to his farm duties. The brooding silence with Martha that had festered since his trip to Hail Ridge melted as they shared terse comments about the weather and their cattle.

On the afternoon of the fourth day after Blake's death, Herb passed by. Standing beside Ethan's main field, they discussed the approaching harvest at inordinate length. When they'd exhausted this subject, Herb sighed.

'I'm heading into Dirtwood,' he said.

'Do you have to?' Ethan coughed, then forced out his next words. 'Maybe Felix is right. Perhaps we should leave Josh and Luke to get bored with hanging around the saloon and move on.'

'Never thought you'd say that.'

Ethan laughed. 'I've been thinking.'

'Glad to hear it.' Herb glanced down the trail and shrugged. 'But I have no choice – provisions are low.'

'Tell me what you need. I'll help.'

Herb smiled. 'Thanks, but I've been thinking too. I've decided I can't hide out, scared every second of the day, worrying that Luke's a-coming. I have to get my life back to normal.'

Ethan nodded. 'I'll come with you. I need provisions too.'

Herb shook his head. 'Don't. Your presence will rile Luke and Josh more than necessary. If I'm on my own, I might return without trouble.'

Ethan sighed, acknowledging Herb's sensible view.

'Luke has plenty of reasons to hate me, but you helped overpower him after he killed Caleb Dalton. He has just as many reasons to hate you.'

Herb jumped into his cart and took a deep breath.

'Perhaps, but I still need provisions.'

'Be careful,' Ethan said.

Herb nodded and shook the reins.

When Herb arrived in Dirtwood, Cooper Rodgers's cart was outside Peter's store. Herb glanced along the road confirming that none of Josh's men was hanging around, and dashed into the store.

'Howdy, Herb,' Cooper said, his face wreathed in his usual smile as he turned from Peter's counter.

Herb forced a smile. 'Howdy to you, Cooper. You delivering? You're back quicker than normal.'

'Yeah. I've been hurrying, what with winter coming.'

'So what's new?'

Cooper patted his paunch, grinning even wider than usual.

'I have plenty to tell you, plenty indeed. In Snakepass Town, a farmer had twins. Two children – who'd have thought it – both identical.'

Herb smiled. 'Two identical children, you say?'

Behind him, the door crashed open and Cooper's wide smile vanished.

'Yeah, two kids,' he whispered.

Herb didn't need to glance back. The long approaching footfalls had to be Luke's.

From his back room Peter glanced in to the store and hung his head. Then he sauntered out, rubbing his hands.

'Luke,' Peter said. 'What can I get you?'

Luke stood beside Cooper and set his hands on his hips.

'I need some things,' Luke said and turned to Cooper. 'But carry on. I like gossip as much as the next man.'

Cooper gulped. 'You might do.'

'Two identical kids would be a fine sight.' Luke glanced at Herb. 'Unless they looked like Herb. Then it'd be enough to put a man off his dinner. What do you say, Herb?'

'If you say so.' Herb hung his head. 'I'll wait outside.'

Luke shrugged. 'You ain't got what you need yet.'

'I ain't, but the air is stale in here.'

Without waiting for a response, Herb sauntered outside and stood on the boardwalk, taking deep breaths.

Some of Josh's men had wandered from the saloon and were leaning against the rail, glaring at him and chuckling amongst themselves. Josh sauntered from the saloon and shared in whatever was amusing them.

To avoid speaking to these men, Herb jumped on his cart. He glanced over his shoulder at the open fields beyond Dirtwood. Then he gripped the reins tight and sat hunched.

Two minutes later, Luke sauntered outside. He leaned back against the doorframe, smiling, until Cooper waddled from the store.

From the corner of his eye, Cooper glanced at Luke, then hurried to his cart. He dragged a bag from the back of his cart, hoisted it on his shoulder, and scurried inside. He repeated this three times, Luke and Josh's men watching him all the time.

When he emerged for the last time, Cooper tipped his hat to Josh and mopped his brow.

Casually Luke pushed from the wall and whispered something to Josh.

With his brow furrowed, Josh nodded. He wandered to Cooper's cart. When Cooper moved to jump on it, he slammed a hand on his arm.

'You is going nowhere,' he muttered.

Cooper gulped. 'I have deliveries to make. I can't stay.'

'Unless I get some answers you ain't going anywhere.'

Cooper shrugged off the arm and mopped his forehead.

'Go on. Ask your questions.'

86

'I'm asking myself how a weasly man like Wiley Douglas gathered the courage to get a message to a lawman.'

'Men do all sorts of things when they're provoked. It ain't my place to comment but from what I saw, you did an awful lot of provoking.'

'Except I've learned that you is interested in gossip. I guess you tell people what's happening in the district. I'm wondering if you might have relayed some gossip about what's happening in Dirtwood.'

Cooper gulped and glanced at Josh's men who peeled from the wall and lined up before him.

'I ain't gossiped about anything here. I'm a businessman and I do nothing to threaten my business. You know that, Josh.'

Josh sauntered in a circle, nodding. He stopped and glared at the sweating Cooper.

'Reckon you probably are just a businessman after all.'

Josh grabbed Cooper's lapels and pulled him forward. He yanked open his jacket and patted the lining. He frowned.

'What you do that for?' Cooper whined.

Josh shrugged and sauntered around Cooper's cart. He patted the provisions bags, then stepped back, a hand raised to his chin. He climbed on to the cart. When he reached the top of the pile of bags, he steadied himself. Still tottering, he glanced at the bags beneath his feet, then glared at Cooper.

Cooper shrugged. 'What are you doing up there?'

Josh paced forward, then held out a hand to stop himself falling.

'I'm risking my life while I wait for you to tell me where it is.'

'Where what is?'

Josh grinned. 'Now there is the question.'

With both hands Josh grabbed a sack and hauled it from the cart. It landed in a cloud of dust.

'Ah come on, Josh,' Cooper said. 'You and I have an understanding. Don't mess up my cart.'

'Then tell me where it is.'

'I don't know what you mean.'

Another bag crashed beside the first and split open. Beans trickled out.

'Ain't got all day to haul these bags, so are you . . .' Josh stood and scratched his head. 'Except it can't be well hidden as you didn't unload too much.'

'Why don't you tell . . .' Cooper sighed as Josh raised a finger and smiled.

'Look what we have here.' Josh prised out a saddle-bag from between two huge bags. 'Reckon this might contain something interesting.'

Cooper gulped and hung his head.

Josh underhanded the saddle-bag to Luke who caught it one-handed.

With his gaze fixed on Cooper's hung head, Luke ripped open the bag. He pulled out a handful of letters and considered the top one. He thrust a finger into one end of the envelope.

Cooper raised his head. 'You can't do that. They're private – just one family writing to another family – nothing that would interest you. But if those letters don't get through, I'll have trouble.'

Luke hurled the letter at Cooper's feet. 'What's

this one about?'

Cooper grabbed the letter and shrugged.

'Don't belittle me.'

As Luke narrowed his eyes, Josh jumped from the cart and chuckled.

'What you don't know, Luke, is our delivery man doesn't know how to read or write.'

With a steady nod, Luke grinned. 'That makes this clearer.'

Luke shuffled through the letters. He stared at each envelope, then dropped it. A pile of discarded letters grew at his feet. Then Luke looked up from a letter and tapped it against his other hand.

'Is that it?' Josh asked.

'Get Peter out here and we'll find out.'

To a grunted command from Josh, Rock dragged Peter from his store.

As Peter emerged, he smoothed his apron.

'What's all . . .' Peter gulped when he saw the pile of letters at Luke's feet.

'This is a letter from Peter,' Luke said. He held it out to Josh.

Josh grabbed the letter, glanced at it, and nodded.

'Tell me what it's about, Peter.'

Peter shrugged. 'It's nothing of interest. I'll read it to you if you insist, but I'm just writing to my sister. She's—'

'Spare me the lies,' Josh muttered.

'That's the truth.'

'This time it might be the truth.' Josh ripped the letter in half and hurled the pieces in the air. 'Wiley got information out of here. Since then, someone else asked for Blake's help. That Ethan was involved, but he wouldn't be the only one.'

'Ethan helped Blake when he got here,' Luke said, 'but Ethan wasn't much use at reading or writing.'

Josh nodded. 'I guess most of the townsfolk can't read or write either and none of them leave Dirtwood much. That don't go for a storekeeper who writes letters to his sister and a tradesman who travels all over the district.'

Peter gulped. He backed into Luke, who grinned at him.

'Where are you going?' Luke whispered.

'Nowhere.'

Luke sighed. 'That's where you're wrong. You're going on a journey. Guess you won't like this one much.'

'Go! Go' Go!' Luke shouted. He nudged Herb in the ribs. 'Who's your money on?'

Herb gulped down the bile rising in his throat.

'I ain't betting on this.'

Luke shrugged and leaned on the rail outside Peter's shop.

The two horses closed fast, Walt and Rock searching for a final spurt as they galloped down the straight stretch of road into Dirtwood.

Most of Josh's men edged forward. They held their hats aloft, waving the horses onwards and shouting for either Walt or Rock.

Herb tried to look away, but he had to watch, hoping that this barbarity would end.

The horses closed on the finishing line. The straining mounts were neck and neck, each rider slapping his hat left and right on his horse's flanks. Behind the horses the bloodied and dusty bodies bounced along the road, flying into the air after each downward crash.

Herb stared at the bodies, hoping that one of them would survive this torture. But as the horses closed, he saw the sickening angles of the limbs and the huge rents ripped down each body. Herb fell to his knees and retched.

'Yes,' Luke cried as Walt's horse edged ahead and crossed the finishing line half a length in the lead.

The extra burst of speed was too much for the following bundle, which ripped in two smearing a long sticky trail down the centre of the road.

Herb looked up to see this. He dropped to his knees again, feeling as if he'd retched up everything he'd eaten in his whole life.

Luke patted him on the back. 'Come on, Herb. I promised them if they survived three circuits of Dirtwood, they could go free. Seems like half of Peter survived. You coming to see how much of Cooper made it?'

With the back of his hand, Herb wiped his mouth. In dazed horror, he watched the riders swing round and return to the saloon.

With Walt having won, Big Dawson organized the settling of the bets.

Still dazed, Herb turned to his cart, shaking his head. As he reached the cart, Luke slammed a hand on his back, buckling him to his knees.

'Guess you didn't enjoy watching that, Herb?'

With his shoulders hunched, Herb stood. 'Nobody

can enjoy watching a man die.'

Luke shrugged. 'Watching someone die is more fun than dying.'

Herb leapt on his cart. He grabbed the reins and glared at Luke.

'If you say so, but I ain't like you.'

Luke snorted. 'You'll learn I'm right. Peter and Cooper got what they deserved. But if you knew what I intend to do to you, you'd slit your own throat to avoid it.'

Herb gulped and glanced at the bloodied bodies in the road.

'Dirtwood won't let you destroy us.'

Luke grinned. 'I won't destroy Dirtwood, just the bits that I have a problem with.'

Herb winced and shook the reins. He swung the cart through Josh's men, scattering them.

The cart bounced as a wheel trundled over something lying in the road. Herb stared straight ahead and cracked the reins, hurtling out of Dirtwood.

CHAPTER 9

'We vote,' Felix said.

'Not yet,' Ethan snapped. 'I ain't had my say.'

Felix sighed. 'We know what you'll say. We don't need to hear from you again.'

Ethan strode to the centre of the barn and banged his fist on Felix's table. As the thud echoed, he swirled round to face the gathered menfolk.

In the reflected light from the oil-lamps on Felix's table, each man's eyes were bright, but they sat hunched and their expressions were grim.

'You *do* need to hear from me. I've a right to speak. Nobody can deny me.'

Ethan glared at each man in turn, daring anyone to argue. When his gaze reached Felix, Felix sighed.

'And you can't deny us *our* rights. The decisions we make bind us, even if we don't agree with them. But you only accept your own rules.'

'I want justice.'

'When Josh and Luke have left and it's safe, we'll get word to the authorities. Our departed friends will get the justice they deserve.'

Ethan set his hands on his hips. 'I meant justice for the living too. I'll do what I think is right to protect my own.'

Felix fingered his gavel, a block of wood, and nodded.

'You'll get no argument on that, but we decided what we'd do about Josh and—'

'And I didn't agree,' Ethan shouted, slamming down his fist again.

'So you fetched a bounty hunter.'

'Nobody said I shouldn't.'

The townsfolk leapt to their feet, all shouting at once.

Felix banged his gavel on the table, calling for order, but it was long minutes before he could make himself heard.

'That's wrong, Ethan,' Felix muttered. 'You took off to avoid facing the truth that nobody shares in your damn-fool schemes.'

Ethan folded his arms and shrugged. 'I had to catch Blake before he left Hail Ridge. I couldn't wait for you to organize a meeting. Sometimes a man has to act.'

'You're right, but you knew what everyone thought about fetching Blake, except you did it anyway.'

Ethan sneered. '*You* decided not to get a bounty hunter and anyone who opposed you was wasting their breath. My only mistake was to ignore your demands.'

Felix shook his head and stared around the assembled townsfolk.

'Ethan, this ain't *my* town and it ain't *your* town. We have democracy, and we ain't accepting anyone living here who don't understand that.'

'Didn't hear too many complaints when Blake ran

94

Josh out of town. If Josh hadn't returned, you'd be telling us that fetching Blake was your idea.'

Felix glanced away, whistling his breath through his teeth.

In the silence, Sam stepped from the group and stood beside Ethan.

'That's enough, Ethan,' he said. 'We should pull together – not argue amongst ourselves.'

Ethan nodded and hung his head a moment. With a great sigh, he rubbed his forehead.

'Sorry, Felix. I ain't tying to take over the decision-making. I just care about Dirtwood.'

'As do I,' Felix whispered.

Ethan turned to face the townsfolk.

'My view is simple. Josh ain't that tough. If we face up to him, he'll run. The rest of his men are hangers-on. They reckon staying keeps them safer than being against him. Blake proved what happens when you face him down. Trouble is – Blake and the sheriff proved what happens when you're on your own. So we band together and show him we ain't intimidated.'

'Except Blake failed,' Felix said. 'Josh returned.'

'He did,' Ethan muttered, slamming his fist into his other hand. 'If we run Josh out of town, maybe killing some of his men, he might return, but only if he thinks he can win. If he knows he has no chance and that we're together, that won't happen.'

Felix sighed. 'We ain't killers. Do you reckon you could kill a man, Ethan?'

Ethan gulped and took a deep breath. He turned to face Felix, but ensured everyone could still see his face.

'Two weeks ago,' he said with his voice low, 'I didn't

know. But this week, I've fired at a number of men. I ain't hit any of them but I could kill any of those men in the saloon. If any of you have doubts, remember the sight of Wiley swinging.'

'Or what was left of Peter and Cooper,' Herb whispered.

Felix fingered his gavel, shaking his head.

'You're avoiding the bigger problem – Luke.'

Ethan shrugged. 'Luke's fast on the draw, but having a fast hand only works when it's one man against one man. Even the fastest draw ain't much use if a dozen men surround him with rifles pointed at his head.'

Grumbled agreements came from the townsfolk. Ethan sought out the few people who'd agreed with him and nodded to them.

Felix lifted a hand. 'In the last week, you've become an expert on gunslingers, Ethan. But your plan will get plenty of people in this barn killed.'

'Better to die at your own choosing defending your kin than at a gunslinger's choosing. You'd sooner die than kill, but I'd sooner die than see you killed. Why won't you treat me in the same way?'

More agreements greeted this comment and Felix banged his gavel for order.

'I do what I think is best, except that ain't what Luke wants. He's caused plenty of trouble but he'll leave before the authorities – who have to be on his tail – find him.'

'That's a big theory.'

Felix threw the gavel on to the table and shrugged.

'It is and it's one we should vote on. I say we avoid trouble. We stay out of Dirtwood while the gunslingers are about and do what we do best – farming.'

To judge the support for Felix, Ethan counted the nods; despite the people who had encouraged him, he had no chance.

Herb jumped to his feet. 'If Ethan's finished, I want to offer a third option.'

Felix nodded. 'That is your right.'

Ethan sat beside the table. 'Yeah, go on. See if you can talk sense into these people.'

Herb paced to the centre of the barn. He coughed and slipped his hat from his head.

'This is my fifteenth year here and I've been thinking about the journey. We travelled for months to find somewhere beyond the ranch owners and when we arrived, we'd passed more land than I ever thought existed. My friend Cooper . . .' Herb hung his head a moment and sighed. 'He used to tell me stories about that land.'

Herb coughed and rubbed at his eyes.

'Take your time, Herb,' Felix said. 'We're as saddened as you are by what happened to Cooper and Peter.'

Herb nodded. 'The way I see it, although we saw plenty of land, we ain't seen a fraction of what's available. There's enough land in this country for every man to build a life for himself and his kin and, as much as I like Dirtwood, it ain't the only place that we could live.'

Herb hung his head and sighed.

Felix glanced at Ethan, who shrugged.

'Are you saying we should leave?' Felix muttered.

Herb nodded, wringing his hat. 'Guess I am.'

'We don't do that.'

'I'm with Felix,' Ethan muttered although he never

97

thought he'd say those words. 'We don't do that.'

Herb coughed. 'You have a right to your opinion, but I want us to vote on leaving.'

Ethan glanced around. He raised his eyebrows as several people nodded and mumbled agreements drifted around the barn, the sound growing. Ethan leapt to his feet.

'This is madness,' he shouted. 'Felix's forbearance is wrong but he's abiding with a principle. Running is plain . . . it's plain cowardice.'

Herb shrugged. 'I have no problem with that. I have a problem with dying.'

In the rising clamour, Ethan grabbed Felix's gavel and slammed it on the table.

'But you don't run. You hold your ground and fight. Even if your way of fighting is to avoid raising your fists, you still stay and hold on to those principles.'

Herb pummelled his hat and it fell from his grip. He bent and picked it up.

'Principles are no use to a dead man,' he murmured.

Felix laughed, the sound hollow. 'Principles are *everything* to a dead man. We live by our beliefs and if necessary, we die by them. That's what freedom means.'

Herb lifted his head and glared at Felix long and hard.

'Last week I would have agreed with you,' he said his voice low and dropping to a barely audible whisper. 'Everything changed when Luke returned. You know that, except you ain't admitting it.,

Felix held Herb's gaze, then hung his head.

With everybody staying quiet, Ethan shook his head.

'Luke changes nothing,' he said. 'The world is full of

his type. So if we move, what happens in the next town?'

'I know,' Herb murmured. 'We move, found a new Dirtwood, and everything is fine. Then one day another Luke rides into town and shoots things up. You'll call for us to run him out of town, Felix will say give him leeway, and we'll decide to get someone else to sort our problem. I've thought this through.'

'You ain't, because the problem's the same and always will be until we fight.'

'I agree and I voted to fight last time, but things changed when Luke arrived. We can stand up to Josh — he's a troublemaker who knows no better. Luke's different. He has a mission and when he's completed it, none of us will be left alive.'

Ethan shook his head. 'If we leave, a man with a mission will come after us. We have to stay and fight.'

Herb shrugged. 'He's an escaped prisoner. Before long someone will come for him.'

'I ain't spending my life looking over my shoulder.'

'I'd sooner do that than die.'

A chorused murmur of approval filled the barn and Ethan banged the gavel on the table. When the barn quieted, Felix held out his hand and Ethan passed the gavel to him.

In sharp succession Felix banged the gavel three times. Then he leapt to his feet and stormed around the table to face Herb.

'This is madness,' Felix said, his voice low and commanding. He gritted his teeth and took a deep breath. 'We won't vote to leave Dirtwood.'

Herb shook his head. 'You're wrong. Before, when we voted on fighting or prevailing, either way we stayed.

If we vote to stay, nothing can stop those who want to leave from going.'

'You can't destroy Dirtwood.'

With both hands held aloft, Ethan stood between them.

'We need to cool down,' Ethan muttered. 'We vote. Then we decide what to do when we hear what everyone thinks.'

Felix glared at Herb, then sighed. 'To stop any more discussion we'll do this on paper.'

Herb and Ethan both nodded and a ripple of nods flowed across the barn.

'There's three choices,' Felix said. 'We either fight, prevail or leave. Make your choice, but choose wisely.'

As Herb sat, Felix and Ethan stared at each other a moment, then busied themselves with distributing paper.

The voting always took time on paper – many of the townsfolk could only mark a cross, Ethan included. While Felix dealt with this, Ethan sat beside Herb and sighed.

'What's really wrong, old friend?' he asked. 'You were tougher than this earlier today.'

Herb drew up and hugged his knees. 'I saw the way Luke looked at me. I heard his threats.'

'What did he say?'

Herb coughed. 'Enough.'

'Herb, Judith chose me over him and that's hurting him.' Ethan stabbed a finger against his chest. 'But whatever his feelings about me, I ain't leaving.'

'You don't know the half of it.'

'Then tell me.'

Herb gave the barest shake of his head and closed his eyes.

For the next ten minutes they voted. Then Felix placed his upturned hat on the table. He tapped his gavel on the table and within seconds, the barn quietened. He drew out and opened the first slip of paper. He glanced at it.

'Prevail,' he said.

The townsfolk drew in their breath as he opened the second slip of paper.

'Leave.'

For each of the votes Felix didn't vary his pace as he slipped his hand into the hat, pulled out the paper, unfolded it, and read the result.

The vote stayed close between prevailing and leaving. Aside from Ethan's vote to fight, nobody had yet added further votes to this choice. After the first six votes, Ethan knew that he wouldn't win tonight and he paced to the wall and joined Sam.

'This will be close,' he said.

'No debate there,' Sam said. 'I voted to fight too, so you still have one more vote to come.'

Ethan patted Sam's shoulder. 'Looks like it's just the two of us with sense.'

Sam gulped. 'Don't want to leave Dirtwood. I still love it here.'

'Nobody can make us leave.'

'Herb's right,' Sam said, snorting. 'If enough want to leave, the ones who are left might have no choice.'

Ethan sighed and turned back to the front table.

'Leave,' Felix said, pulling out the fourth such vote.

CHAPTER 10

'You staring at that drink all evening?' Josh asked.

Luke fingered his whiskey-glass and smiled.

'Ain't done anticipating it yet.'

'I'd drink it. Then you can anticipate your second whiskey.'

Luke shrugged and swirled the whiskey around, letting the acrid aroma fill his nostrils.

'Thinking about having this drink in Dirtwood's saloon kept me sane for seven years. It's doing the same now.'

Josh poured himself a large drink. 'And I need something to keep me sane too. After what we did to Peter and Cooper, nobody will hurry back into Dirtwood.'

'Yeah. Things were quiet before, but now . . .'

Josh sneered and gulped his whiskey. 'Pity. A man can play just so many games of poker.'

Luke nodded and poured a small puddle of whiskey on to the bar.

'I didn't return to Dirtwood to watch your men play poker either.'

'So what did you return for?'

'Came for three things – a drink at this saloon, to see someone I used . . .' Luke knocked the whiskey-glass to the floor.

Josh chuckled. 'If you keep knocking those glasses away, you'll anticipate that drink for a long time.'

Luke sighed, his flash of anger gone.

'Yeah, and I won't see that someone again.'

Josh shrugged. He stared at Luke a moment, then poured himself another drink. He waved the bottle at Luke, but Luke shook his head. 'What was the third thing you came for?'

'You know about that one.' Luke grinned. 'Revenge.'

Josh leaned forward. 'That word's more interesting than poker, whiskey – even women.'

'Yeah. I've had plenty of time to think. I can be inventive.'

Josh laughed. 'Seen that. Mighty fine idea dragging those men around the town until they fell apart.'

'And I have other ideas.' Luke turned to Josh and smiled. 'Except you can't stay here if you want to help.'

Josh grinned and glanced around the saloon.

'I like the sound of this already.'

Ethan stormed into his house. He ripped his jacket from his shoulders and hurled it at the wall for it to slide to the floor.

With his shoulders hunched, he stood before the empty fireplace and kicked at a log.

Martha rose from the table and stood beside him with her arms folded. When Ethan glanced her way, she smiled.

'Things not go your way, then?' she asked.

'Go my way?' Ethan roared. 'They didn't listen. They didn't . . .'

Martha laughed.

On realizing that she was baiting him, Ethan forced a smile.

'I'm sorry,' he said, 'but they didn't listen to sense.'

'You mean they didn't listen to you.'

'That's what I said.'

'What did they decide?'

'To sum up two hours' talking – we ain't fighting.'

Martha shrugged her shawl around her tighter.

'As I expected. But you have to accept town decisions.'

'That ain't the worst of it.' Ethan strode across their room and slumped in his chair. He looked at Dale and Sarah, who sat hunched in blankets. 'It's late. The children should be in bed.'

Martha shrugged. 'They should, but they don't sleep when you're out. I said they could wait until you got home.'

'I'm home.'

Without further word, Martha shepherded the children into their room. They went without complaint.

When Martha returned, she sighed. 'What's so bad you couldn't say it before the children?'

Ethan rubbed his forehead, drying the sweat that'd come when Herb had suggested his mad idea.

'We also voted on leaving Dirtwood. Seven families wanted to.'

'Leave?' Martha shouted, throwing her hand to her mouth. 'They can't. We just—'

Ethan lifted a hand. 'I know, but something changed tonight. Unless we resolve this soon, more families will change their minds and the vote will be to go.'

Martha set her hands on her hips. 'We ain't going.'

'I know, but—'

'But what? We ain't going.'

Ethan glanced at his hands and nodded.

'Like you said, we agreed that we'd abide by town decisions. It's democracy.'

'Democracy doesn't mean that. It means fighting for what you believe in. It means never having to . . .' Martha sighed. 'I guess you said this earlier.'

'I said it and more.'

Martha strode to Ethan's side and knelt beside his chair. She rested a hand on his.

'Nobody can make us leave, but I suppose the ones that want to leave will go.'

With his other hand, Ethan reached over and squeezed Martha's hand.

'Ain't so sure yet. Felix can be persuasive. Usually I'm on the receiving end of his tongue but he's admirable when he's on your side. After the vote, he argued and argued. In the end everyone pretty much agreed with him that as the town decision was to stay, nobody could leave on their own.'

'Pretty much?'

'Herb ain't convinced. He's petrified. He reckons Luke will kill him. Before the week ends, he'll pack and nothing will persuade him to stay. I hope when he goes, it'll convince everyone else that that ain't the way.'

Martha sat round to look into the fire. 'You sound unsure.'

'I am, but what can I do? Getting Blake didn't work, so nobody will accept me acting on my own, and nobody will support me in taking on Josh. I'm on my own.'

Martha turned from the fire and looked at him, smiling. 'You have us.'

'I know.' Ethan gulped and slipped his hand from Martha's. 'I'm sorry, but I need something more.'

'What does that mean?' she snapped.

To avoid Martha's firm gaze Ethan pushed to his feet and sauntered to the shutters. He pressed his head against them letting the rough wood prickle his hot forehead. With no words coming, he leaned back and flung the shutters wide.

Outside the darkness was absolute but as he stared, a movement caught his gaze.

He ducked and grabbed his rifle.

'What is it?' Martha muttered.

Ethan lifted a finger to his lips and slipped to the door.

'Don't worry,' he whispered. 'I'll be careful.'

He flung the door wide and swung outside. He stood. Then he tensed and dashed back in.

'Have they come for us?' Martha asked, clutching her shawl tight about her neck.

Ethan gulped. 'Nope. It's worse. There's a fire.'

When Ethan and Martha reached Felix's farm, the blaze had gutted the house and was ripping through the barn.

Every few minutes more people arrived to help ferry buckets in a steady line from the well to the barn, but the flames licked ever higher.

With his tread heavy, Ethan grabbed a bucket and joined in the line. He was about to ask if Felix had escaped, but then he saw the row of covered bodies – Felix, July and their son, Roger.

Ethan closed his eyes. Moisture ran down his

cheeks and not all of it produced by the acrid smoke churning from the buildings.

Sam pushed into the line of bucket-passers beside Ethan and nodded towards the bodies.

'I got here too late,' he shouted. 'They were dead.'

'Who got the bodies out?'

'Felix got July out, but she died before anybody could help. When Felix returned for Roger, the heat was too much. I got in too but I could only get their bodies out.'

'This was no accident,' Ethan muttered.

'No argument there.' Sam rubbed his blackened face. 'But this is the end. You can see the look in everyone's eyes.'

Ethan spat on the ground. 'I know. We'll fight.'

Sam shook his head. 'No. We'll leave. Nobody will want to carry on after this.'

'To hell with you all,' Ethan snapped and shouted encouragement to the line of bucket-carriers, spurring them on in the hopeless attempt to quell the fire.

'Luke, you ain't like Josh,' Herb muttered with a deep gulp.

'Guess we'll find out if you're right,' Luke said. He grinned and beckoned Rock to pull the rope and hoist Herb higher.

With his feet just touching the floor and his arms high above his head, Herb winced. He stared around his home. Josh and six of his men leaned against his walls, their faces gleaming and eager.

'What did you do to Felix?' Herb whispered.

'Felix suffered the worst death of all. He watched his family die.'

Herb gulped. 'You'll rot in hell for that.'

Luke shrugged and edged his knife nearer to Herb's face.

'Maybe, but I have to test a theory. I'm wondering if Felix *did* suffer the worst death there is. Guess you'll tell me if I'm right.'

'Don't, Luke. We were friends.'

Luke nodded. 'We were. So are you telling me that it was all Felix's and Peter's fault?'

'Would it help?'

Luke ran a finger down the edge of the knife.

'Probably not. Felix told me you and Peter were to blame before we started the fire and it didn't help him.'

Herb sighed. 'Then I'll tell you the truth.'

Luke shrugged and edged the knife closer to Herb's right eye.

'You will. Before too long you'll tell me anything I want to stop me, but I ain't stopping.'

'This will be fun,' Josh gibbered from the corner of the room.

Luke sneered. 'This ain't fun. I'm doing what I have to do.'

'Yeah, but it don't stop us having fun.'

Luke lowered his head a moment.

'Luke,' Herb said, keeping his voice as calm as he could. 'You ain't like Josh. He's an animal. He enjoys seeing people suffer. You've done your share of suffering and you're trying to make sense of it all. You got it wrong so far, but you can change. I knew the man you once were.'

Luke nodded and lowered the knife. He swung it round to grip it underhand.

'I enjoyed anticipating killing Peter and Felix more than doing it. You have to die, but I can make it quick.'

Herb tried to meet Luke's eyes, but Luke stared at the

108

knife. Then Luke lunged, the knife thrusting forward.

Herb closed his eyes, but the pain didn't come. He opened his eyes.

Josh had clamped his hand over Luke's arm.

'What you doing?' Josh shouted. 'You told us about the fun we'd have with Herb, but you're finishing him with one thrust.'

Luke shrugged, letting the knife fall from his hand.

'Ain't seeing much point in it any more.'

Josh grinned and lifted the knife. 'Sounds as if Luke's gone squeamish. That don't go for me.'

With his grin widening, Josh edged the knife to Herb's face.

At Felix's farm, the townsfolk fought for the next hour. Practically everybody joined in the fight, although the flames would clearly win tonight.

In the next hour, the exhausted townsfolk relented from their battle. This left Ethan and Martha dashing back and forth hurling water at the rippling flames until Martha collapsed from exhaustion and two minutes later, Ethan slipped in the mud. He lay and couldn't summon the energy to rise.

Sam sloshed through the mud and pulled him to his feet.

'It's over, Ethan.'

'No it ain't,' Ethan shouted. 'We have to fight. We have to—'

Sam shook his head. 'Have respect. This ain't the time for speeches. We'll meet in an hour. Martha says we can use your barn. We'll decide what to do then.'

'We'll decide to fight,' Ethan whispered.

'Perhaps.' Sam sighed. 'But I'd start packing if I were you.'

'Never,' Ethan shouted. As the townsfolk backed, he tried to catch as many people's gaze as he could. Then he rubbed his forehead.

'Sam,' he said. 'Is Herb here?'

Sam glanced around, then shrugged. 'Ain't seen him.'

Ethan tipped back his hat. 'His farm is the nearest to Felix's. He ought to be here.'

With a hollow laugh, Sam wrung out his jacket, freeing a shower of water.

'Perhaps he's asleep. You know what Herb's like.'

Ethan rubbed his soot-coated face and sighed.

'Maybe. Let's check on him.'

He sought out Martha, who clutched his rifle. She opened her mouth but then closed it and handed him his rifle.

Ethan and Sam dashed across the fields to Herb's farm. Others followed but they left them behind in their headlong dash.

No inside lights illuminated Herb's farmhouse, as Ethan had expected, but even so, something about the darkened windows battered at his nerves.

They halted outside and glanced at each other. The moon was up, the crescent providing enough light to see most of the house, the dying light from the fire at Felix's farm also flickering across the sod walls.

Without a word, they scouted around and found a trail of shod hoofprints.

Ethan gulped. Herb hadn't shod his horse.

With his eyes wide, Sam looked up from the prints

and nodded. Using as much stealth as possible, they edged to the door.

Ethan counted to three, then kicked open the door. The door slammed back against the wall and they stood on either side of it.

When long seconds had passed, Ethan noticed a sound above the hammering of his heart. From inside, a slow creaking echoed. He gulped and glanced in through the doorway, then spun back against the wall.

'See anything?' Sam mouthed.

Ethan nodded and stood straight. 'Yeah, Herb's dead.'

Sam hung his head a moment, then turned into the doorway. He gulped and dropped to his knees to retch.

Ethan patted him on the back. Coming along the trail were a dozen or so townsfolk. Ethan hoisted Sam to his feet and wandered down the path to meet them.

'Sorry, folks,' he said. 'We were too late. They got Herb. He's dead.'

'How did he die?' Morgan asked.

Ethan ran his arm over his forehead. 'He didn't die easy. Guess we didn't hear his screams over the noise of the fire. Someone get me a sack and I'll get him out.'

'You want help?'

Ethan took a deep breath. 'Nope. It won't do anyone any good to see him. I'll deal with it.'

While everyone hung their heads, Sam sidled through the group. Morgan had brought his cart and he returned with a large square of cloth.

'Come on, Ethan,' Sam said. 'I'll help.'

Ethan nodded and they paced to Herb's house, their steps heavy and slowing with each pace.

CHAPTER 11

'You look bored,' Josh muttered. 'Why not join in the poker-game?'

Luke shrugged over the bar and slipped the whiskey-glass closer to him.

'Ain't interested.'

Josh sighed and leaned on the bar beside him.

'You telling me what's wrong?'

'Doubt you'd understand.'

Josh grabbed a whiskey-bottle from the bar. He poured himself a large drink and without asking, added more whiskey to Luke's untouched glass.

'I've heard it all before. Trouble is my speciality. I hand out plenty but I have my share of problems.'

'Anticipating what I'd do when I left prison kept me sane, but the reality ain't matched the anticipation.' Luke sighed and swirled his full glass of whiskey. 'The woman I returned to see is dead and killing the men that put me away ain't satisfied me.'

'Can see why that might tear a man up.'

Luke poured the excess whiskey from his glass to create a pool on the bar. With the flat of his hand, he swiped it away and replaced the half-filled glass before him.

'Drinking this whiskey is all I have left to anticipate. After that, what's left for me?'

Josh grinned. In a prolonged swallow he gulped his whiskey and smacked his lips.

'That's easy. You have another whiskey, then another. Soon none of it matters. There'll be other women and other men to kill.' Josh held up his empty glass. 'And plenty more whiskey.'

'Yeah, but that's all there is. Just more of the same and none of it as good as the first time.'

Josh laughed and sloshed another shot of whiskey into his glass. 'Sounds like a good life to me.'

'Not to me. I want something else, just I don't know what it is.' Luke ran a finger around the top of his whiskey-glass. 'When I know what it is, I'll drink this whiskey. Until then, I'll anticipate drinking it.'

'I've an idea.' Josh leaned forward breathing whiskey fumes over Luke. 'I've had enough of that Ethan. He was the one who stole your woman.'

'He didn't steal her,' Luke roared, slamming his fist on the bar. 'Him doing right by her is all I ever wanted.'

Josh shrugged and leaned back. 'But you returned for her.'

'I didn't. I knew she was long past wanting me. I just wanted to see her again and know that she was happy.'

Luke sneered and lifted his hand to swipe the whiskey-glass to the floor, but Josh grabbed his arm.

'Don't want you wasting more good whiskey.'

As Josh took the glass and placed it beside his glass, Luke nodded and pushed back from the bar.

'Then I'll get some fresh air.'

'Want company?'

'Nope. Some questions need answering.'

Josh grinned and hoisted his gunbelt high. 'I like asking questions.'

Luke paused at the swing-doors. 'So do I, but this time I'm providing the answers.'

'When will you back?' Josh shouted.

With his shoulders hunched high, Luke pushed through the swing-doors and stormed into the night.

'We will fight,' Ethan roared, showering phlegm over the table as he slammed down his fist again.

He gazed around the barn, trying to meet anyone's eye.

'You ain't listening,' Morgan said. 'We've voted. Sixteen say leave. One says prevail. One says fight.'

Ethan looked to Sam but Sam shook his head.

'I'm sorry, Ethan,' Sam said. 'This is over. I voted to stay, but . . .'

'But nothing. You saw what they did to Herb.'

Sam gulped and hung his head. 'I did. And I never want to see another person die. I ain't a coward and they ain't running me off my land, but I ain't lowering myself to the level of animal that can do that to a man.'

Ethan slammed his fist on the table again, the wood splintering beneath the blow.

'You heard the word. You're cowards. Every last one of you, wanting to run when faced by the likes of Josh and Luke.'

Morgan shook his head. 'Perhaps. You and Sam are the only dissenters. Sam's agreed to accept the majority

114

decision. You'll respect that decision too or we'll throw you out.'

Ethan gritted his teeth, then flung himself to the ground. With a glare at Morgan, he drew his legs to his chin and stared at his barn wall.

By degrees the conversation calmed and in low voices everyone debated the escape plan, a grim practicality taking over.

The plan they hatched without Ethan's help was simple.

They'd avoid Dirtwood and tend their animals. But the children and womenfolk would stay inside and pack the minimum they needed. An hour after sunset tomorrow, they'd pack their carts and tether their animals. Then they'd head for the Oregon Trail, making as much speed as possible.

They'd discuss how far to go another day.

In a lull, Ethan noticed that everyone was looking at him. He shrugged.

'Pardon?' he said.

'You're quiet,' Morgan said. 'Do you want to add to those plans?'

'Yeah, I have something to add.' Ethan climbed to his feet. 'I ain't leaving.'

Morgan sighed. 'We *are* leaving. Accept that and help us.'

'I have accepted it and I intend to help you escape. But the way I see it, there's another option. You can leave, but I can stay and fight.'

'What?' Sam shouted. The question echoed through the barn.

'You heard. You go. I stay.'

115

Sam chuckled. He strode across the barn and patted Ethan's shoulder.

'I know what you're doing and it's a good try, but shaming us into fighting is wrong. Everybody has decided, and tomorrow we're leaving. We ain't happy for you to get yourself killed. We just want you to swallow your pride. We can build a new life somewhere else, and we'd like you to join us.'

Ethan shook his head. 'You have me wrong. I ain't shaming you. I know you're hell-bent on leaving, but you've forgotten something. To escape, we need a distraction.'

Sam scratched his chin. 'Possibly.'

'No possibly about it. If I can distract them and take some with me, I can buy the rest of you enough time to escape.'

'That's madness.'

'It ain't.' Ethan sighed. 'While you're leaving, I'll ride into Dirtwood. I'll shoot up Josh's men – hopefully Luke getting a bullet – and hightail it out of there, heading east. With the fastest horse, I can lead them a merry chase. When they tire, they'll return to Dirtwood. They'll find you're long gone and their horses will be in no state to chase you. Meanwhile, I'll head north and swing round to join you.'

As a round of nodding waved around the room, Ethan smiled.

'Looks like you is getting support, Ethan,' Sam said, 'provided you can do it.'

'I can but I ain't finished. I accept we leave, but abandoning everything we've built here is like chopping off your leg because you have an itch.'

116

'Ethan, we've decided.'

'I know I've lost that battle, but we can keep our options open. We're abandoning our crops. Without them, life will be hard this winter. I suggest we head west and hide in the hills. Then in two weeks, I'll return and scout around. If Josh and Luke have gone, we can return to Dirtwood. But if they stay, we can find somewhere else to live.'

Sam smiled. 'Now you're working with us, you're speaking sense. What does everyone think to that?'

'Think to what?' someone roared as the barn door slammed open.

All eyes turned to the door. Luke stood in the doorway, his long legs wide and his hand resting on his gunbelt.

'Nothing,' Ethan muttered.

Luke grinned. 'Sounds like something to me.'

Sam strode into the centre of the barn. 'If you want, Luke, you can join us.'

Luke nodded. 'That's neighbourly of you.'

'We could use an extra pair of hands.' Sam sneered. 'You should remember how to bring in the harvest. Dirtwood pulls together and with you and your thugs killing half of the town, we have our work cut out.'

Luke glanced at his hands. 'Never took to the farming life. I'll decline that offer.'

'Then you can return to taking orders from Josh and we'll return to our planning.'

Luke spat on the ground. 'You won't. I'm here to talk to Ethan, provided he ain't too pig-headed to listen.'

Ethan snorted. He stormed past Sam but Sam grabbed him and pulled him back.

117

'Don't let Luke goad you,' Sam whispered.

'He ain't,' Ethan muttered. 'I'm goaded enough already. But he's right. We have to sort this.'

Luke nodded. 'That's why I'm here.'

Sam stood beside Ethan and glared at Luke, but Ethan pushed him away.

'I ain't looking for help,' Ethan said. 'We've decided on how we're bringing in the harvest. Best you return to your farms. Luke and me have some talking to do.'

Everyone jumped to their feet and filed outside. Luke stood beside the barn door and smiled at each person as they passed.

Several people spat at Luke's boots. The rest scurried past. Luke kept smiling.

Ethan lifted a hand to Sam's ear. 'When you're outside, tell everyone we're leaving tonight.'

'We agreed on tomorrow,' Sam whispered.

'Yeah, but with Luke coming here, this is building to an end. I reckon we don't have a tomorrow. We go now or we never go. I'll deal with Luke. You deal with our people.'

Sam frowned, then nodded. 'Leave it to me – and don't give him any leeway.'

Sam was the last to leave, dashing past Luke without looking at him. Then Luke and Ethan were alone.

'Guess you've looked forward to killing me,' Ethan muttered.

Luke shrugged. 'Nope. You said you were a good husband to Judith. She deserved the best and if she got that, I have no problem with you.'

'Yeah. She got the best.'

Luke strode from the wall to the centre of the barn and stood before Ethan.

'I know,' he murmured, kicking at the ground. 'Life with me would have been rough. I was always going to turn out bad.'

Ethan rubbed his chin and considered Luke's hunched stance.

'Why are you here?'

Luke scuffed more earth. 'Because you have a problem with me.'

'I ain't. I know the truth about you and Judith.' Ethan folded his arms. 'You feel guilty because she cared for you more than you cared for her. Except she was too blind to see that.'

Luke lifted a finger. 'Don't speak wrong of her.'

'I ain't. She came to her senses and picked me, and I know how much that hurt you.'

'We know the truth ain't that simple.'

'Maybe. So what are we doing about it?'

Luke smiled. He unhooked his gunbelt and let it fall to the ground.

'We fought over Judith before. She ain't around, but it's time to fight over her one last time.'

'I ain't fighting over her again. I made my peace with her death long ago. You should do the same. Then you can move on and leave us alone.'

Luke raised his fists. 'Shall I tell you some things you never found out about Judith? Shall I tell you about the time we went down to the creek and—'

'No,' Ethan roared and charged across the barn.

With his head down, he clattered into Luke forcing him back against the barn wall. The wall shook with the impact, all wind blasting from Luke's chest as he slid to the ground.

Ethan backed, his fists raised.

Luke looked up, smiling. 'Seems I have your attention.'

Luke leapt to his feet and raised his fists. Walking sideways, he wheeled around Ethan.

Many childhood scuffles with Luke flashed through Ethan's mind. He smiled. Luke had won them, but Luke had languished in prison for the last seven years and Ethan had worked on the land. He raised his fists higher.

'Come on. Take a shot.'

Luke nodded. He danced forward and slammed a fist into Ethan's guts.

As Ethan had tensed, he avoided wincing and smiled at Luke.

'I'm tougher than the boy you used to beat. You're about to find out how tough.'

With solid force, Ethan drove his fist into Luke's side. He followed it with a flurry of blows to his chin and cheeks.

Luke tried to counter-attack but Ethan's blows came fast, until Luke stumbled and landed on his back. He lay a moment and rubbed his chin.

'You *have* changed. You could never hurt me before.' Luke jumped to his feet. 'Trouble is. I've changed too.'

Ethan shrugged and paced in to knock him down again. In the same style as before he drove his fist into Luke's side, then swung up his other fist, but a sharp pain shot up Ethan's leg as Luke stamped on his instep.

Ethan staggered back, to receive another kick to the thigh and a third to his stomach as he fell forward. He floundered on the ground and looked up as Luke's boot slammed down towards his outstretched hand. Ethan snatched the hand away just as the boot crunched into the ground.

Luke swung his other boot around aiming for Ethan's face.

Ethan dropped back, the boot grazing his shoulder. As his arm numbed, he reached for Luke's left boot but Luke swung over him and stabbed down with two fingers, aiming for his eyes.

To deflect the blow Ethan threw his arm up, the hand jabbing into his forearm. Then Luke grabbed Ethan's hair and yanked his head back. Ethan rolled over, his head thudding into the ground.

As he lay dazed, Luke slammed his boot into Ethan's guts and walked over him, blasting the wind from him.

Ethan rolled into a ball, trying to avoid the next blow while he regained his breath, but it didn't come.

Luke sauntered past him and leaned on the barn wall.

'You ready to go again yet?' he asked.

With a tentative hand, Ethan rubbed his stomach and gulped in a deep breath.

'Guess you've learnt how to fight dirty.'

'*That* wasn't dirty.' Luke shrugged. 'You may have grey hairs in that fine, black head of hair, but you're stronger than me. And you can probably take a punch better than I can. But a man doesn't survive seven years of prison unless he knows how to defend himself. And that don't involve following any rules. I was only fighting fair before out of an old friendship. If you want to carry on, I'll stop playing fair and get real dirty.'

Ethan rolled to his knees and pushed to his feet.

'I ain't scared.'

'I know, but you have two minutes before I start doing permanent damage and two more minutes before you end up dead. What do you want to do?'

Ethan spat on his hands. 'I'd back my fair ways more than your dirty ways any day.'

'That ain't a bet I'd take.' Luke beckoned. 'Come on, if you ain't had enough.'

Ethan shrugged. Then he charged. Aiming to flatten Luke with one blow, he swung his fist round at Luke's cheek.

In a casual gesture, Luke swayed back and when he swayed forward, he drove a fist deep into Ethan's lower gut, following up with a knee that drove even lower.

With his insides turned to water, Ethan doubled over the blow to receive a second jab to the throat and a flailing elbow to the side of the head. He dropped to his knees and shook the blood from his eyes just in time to see a boot heading for his face.

Then blackness stole over him.

CHAPTER 12

Luke stood over Ethan's body. Anger still coursed through his veins and he pulled back his boot ready to kick Ethan again.

'Stop!' a woman demanded.

Luke spun round. Martha stood in the barn doorway, a rifle held to her shoulder.

With his hands held wide, Luke smiled. 'You can't fire that thing. It's awful big for a dainty woman like you.'

'If you try anything, I can test that.'

Luke sighed and nodded. 'You have more guts than anyone else in Dirtwood. You make a fine woman for Ethan.'

'Quit talking and start backing.'

Luke backed to the wall and stood over his gunbelt. He glanced at it. To Martha's nod, he grabbed the gunbelt, but held it at arm's length.

'You letting me go?'

'Yeah,' Martha said. Then she shrugged. 'But what happened here? You have no compunction about killing, but you're different with Ethan.'

'You ain't interested in what happened here seven years ago.'

Martha shrugged. 'I've heard other people's versions, so I can hear yours. No matter what I hear, it ain't changing my view.'

'Sounds a fair offer.' Luke sighed and rubbed the back of his neck. His eyes glazed for a moment. 'Ethan and I were the only boys amongst the pioneers who headed west. So we had to be friends, except I was always getting into trouble and Ethan was always getting into being sensible.'

'So far, so believable.'

'My parents didn't make it through the first winter and so I stayed with Caleb Dalton. He was a mean son of a bitch but he doted over his daughter Judith. His affection went to her and every beating came to me.'

Martha snorted. 'How tragic for you. Seems you have an excuse for all the killing.'

Luke smiled. 'I deserve that sarcasm. But I meant that Judith deserved it. She was like a sister to me, except as we grew we didn't view each other as kin. Judith didn't have many choices for suitors and it came down to Ethan, the dullest man in Dirtwood, or me.'

'Guess I know who she chose.'

'You can guess, but all that matters is that Caleb decided that she'd chosen me. He tried to run me out of town. When I wouldn't go, he called me out of the saloon.' Luke wrapped his gunbelt around his waist, then held his hands high. 'Caleb had stopped beating me a good year past when I got too big, so I ignored him. I continued drinking with my three new friends who were teaching me how a young man can spend

124

an evening in a saloon.'

'Those drinking buddies were Herb, Peter and Felix?'

'Yup. They said I had to face his challenge, so I put down my half-drunk glass of whiskey and borrowed Felix's gun. I went outside. I'd shot animals and I knew I was quick on the draw, but I didn't know how fast. Caleb went for his gun, but I shot him before his gun had left its holster. I threw my gun back to Felix and went back into the saloon, but I never finished my drink. I stayed in a daze for a month. Couldn't believe I'd shot a man. That was it until Marshal Devine arrived.'

Martha nodded. 'You saying that Marshal Devine saw things different to you?'

With the toe of his boot, Luke kicked at a clod of earth.

'I'm saying that the whole evening was different. Everybody's stories matched except they didn't describe the evening I remembered. Without too many questions, Marshal Devine believed them and so did the judge. The next I knew, I was in prison.'

From the strain of holding the rifle rigid, Martha flexed her shoulders, then dropped it to her side.

'I can't argue with your story, but I knew Felix. He believed in peace and telling the truth.'

'Perhaps he formed his views after he lied and put me away.'

Martha shrugged. 'If you were half the man Felix was, you'd have given him a chance to make amends. But as he's dead, we won't know the truth of what he did or why he did it.'

Luke nodded. 'I've thought about that and I know the answer. He was scared. He figured a man who could draw a gun like I did wouldn't become a farmer. So he removed me.'

Martha sighed and patted her rifle against her leg.

'I can't judge you, but what you've done here is wrong.'

With an angry lunge, Luke spat on the ground.

'You can say that when you ain't lived in prison. Seven years behind bars does something to a man. Every night I kept sane by anticipating the pain I'd inflict on the rats that put me there, and that's what I've done.'

'That ain't justice.'

Luke slammed his fist against his thigh. 'Perhaps, but if they'd told the truth, my life would have been different. I'd probably be a farmer, fighting on your side to protect the town against Josh, but I ain't. Felix, Herb and Peter saw to that. I wasn't the gunslinger they thought I was, but that night they made me into one.'

Martha lowered her head a moment. 'You've killed the men who you reckoned wronged you, so what're you going to do now?'

Luke rubbed his forehead. 'Suppose I'll make a new life for myself. Just like you're doing.'

Martha gulped. 'I don't know what you mean.'

'I ain't stupid. You're escaping.'

'We ain't. We're bringing in the harvest tomorrow.'

'No you ain't. You're running. That's appropriate. Dirtwood deserves to die for what it did to me.'

'Just go.' Martha lifted her rifle to her shoulder and gestured to the barn door. 'I've heard enough of your whining.'

Luke nodded and swung round. With Martha two steps behind, he strode from the barn to his horse.

As they strode across the scrubby grass, Martha glanced to her side. Dale stood beside the barn.

'What's happening, Ma?' he asked.

'Nothing,' Martha said. 'Go back to the house.'

'Is Pa all right?'

'He is. Return this instant.'

Dale nodded. He backed, then turned and strode to the house.

'Wait!' Luke roared.

Dale stopped and looked at him without fear.

'What's wrong, sir?'

'Nothing, boy. What's your name?'

'I'm Dale Craig, sir.'

'Go, Dale!' Martha shouted. 'Me and this man have some business.'

Dale glanced between them, then wandered to the house, Luke watching his every step.

Luke tore his gaze away. 'He one of yours?'

'Nope.' Martha frowned. 'He's Ethan's and Judith's, as is their youngest, Sarah. Ethan and me ain't had kin yet.'

Luke nodded. 'He seems mighty tall and grown-up for one so young.'

'Out here living is harsh. It does that to you.'

'He must be at least five years old.'

'He's six.'

Luke nodded. 'Does he have a birthday soon? If I'm still around, I could buy him something.'

'He don't want anything you could give him.'

'Handsome, fair-haired child like that deserves a present.'

127

'And he'll get one from his pa and his new ma.'

Luke grabbed his horse's reins and swung into the saddle. He glanced at the house.

'Not everyone deserves what they get.'

At a steady gait, Luke rode from the house. Martha watched his form disappear into the dark. She watched the trail until she saw Luke silhouetted against the night sky on the next ridge.

Then he was gone.

Martha took a deep breath and strode into the barn. She patted Ethan's shoulder.

'Let's get this new life started,' she whispered as she shook him, but he remained unconscious. 'There's nothing for us here.'

At a slow trot, Luke rode along the trail from Dirtwood, heading south. Ahead the prairies beckoned. The darkened fields passed him, the ghostly outlines of the crops swaying in the wind.

Luke stared at the crops, his jaw clenched tight.

'I'd never have been a farmer,' he whispered. 'I'd have taken off and sought my freedom. Judith understood.'

With each clumped pace, he slowed until he drew his horse to a halt. He glanced around.

The acrid smell of burning was everywhere but it couldn't mask the other sweet smells of the prairies that he'd remembered through his seven years in prison. The breeze rustled through the crops. In the distance the occasional cry sounded as Dirtwood's townsfolk prepared for their flight into the hills.

Without thinking, Luke swung his horse around and

headed back down the trail. At his steady pace, he'd clumped for 200 yards before he realized that he was heading back to Dirtwood.

Luke licked his lips and smiled. He hurried to a trot.

'What? Where? Let me ...' Ethan muttered and jumped up as he awoke.

He swayed back and forth. He winced but then realized that he was swaying because he was in the back of his cart.

Ethan swung to his knees. He looked around. A block of carts surrounded him, their outlines faint in the blackness of a cloudy night.

'Martha,' he said.

At the front of the cart, Martha swung around.

'How are you feeling?'

Ethan rubbed his forehead. 'Awake.'

'That's about all we can ask for. Lie back and rest.'

'How long has it been?'

'A few hours. Luke sure knocked you out.'

Ethan rubbed his chin, fingering the bruising. 'Is everyone with us?'

'Relax. Sam's organized us just fine. People are scouting around, but so far, nobody is following us. By dawn we'll be miles from Dirtwood and when Josh notices we're gone, he'll never find us.'

'He can follow trails.'

Martha laughed. 'All cared for. Don't worry. Everyone's managing just fine without you. Rest until you're less groggy. We want you fit to face the next few weeks.'

Ethan blinked twice and stretched, feeling only grogginess. He climbed to his feet.

Dale and Sarah smiled at him in the back of the cart.

'Your pa is fine,' he said.

'We know,' Dale said.

Ethan climbed into the front of the cart.

'What happened after Luke knocked me out?' Ethan asked.

Martha muttered to herself, then shrugged.

'Nothing. Beating you was all he needed.'

'But he'll warn Josh that we're going.'

'He said he won't.'

Ethan sighed and glanced back and forth. They were towards the back of the train of carts.

'You can't believe anything Luke says.'

'I believed him about this. He said he'd had the revenge he wanted. He had no argument with anyone else so after fighting you, he headed south. I reckon he'll try and enjoy himself until they string him up.'

'You don't know him. He ain't to be trusted.'

Martha shrugged. She held the reins in both hands and turned in her seat to face Ethan.

'He sounded different to what I expected from a man that has killed so many other men. He looked at Dale and there was a look in his eyes. Then he said he was leaving and—'

'You what?' Ethan jumped to his feet and swayed with the sudden movement.

'Sit, Ethan.'

'Sam,' he hollered. 'Get back here.'

Sam glanced over his shoulder, then peeled from the front of the train of carts.

'Nice to see you awake, Ethan,' he said when Ethan's

cart drew alongside. 'Luke sure knocked you cold.'

Ethan shrugged his jacket closed. 'Sam, I need your horse.'

'I'm scouting around while you rest. When you're better, you can take over. That'll probably be tomorrow, so just take it easy.'

'Tomorrow is too late. I need your horse to return to Dirtwood.'

'No,' Martha shouted, grabbing Ethan's arm.

Ethan ignored her grip and stared at Sam.

'I said I'd return for our escape plan, and nothing has changed. If Luke's warned Josh we're leaving, I'll lead him away. If Luke ain't warned him, I'll shoot up the town and head east. I'll lead him from us, then head back.'

Sam shook his head. 'That's too risky.'

Martha sobbed, strangulating the sound in an instant.

'Sam's right,' she said. 'We've escaped and we're alive and that's the best we could have hoped for.'

Ethan sighed and turned back to Martha. 'I have no intention of getting myself killed, but I have every intention of ensuring we live.'

Martha shook her head. 'Despite everything, I've backed you on your mad schemes, but not this time. Just stay with us and do whatever you think you have to do to defend your kin, but don't leave.'

Ethan breathed deeply, but every turn of the wheels took him further from Dirtwood.

'I'm sorry,' he whispered. He turned to Sam who, with a last glance at Martha, nodded.

Sam swung his horse from the cart.

Martha stared straight ahead. She gripped the reins as if letting go of them was letting go of Ethan. Then, with an angry shake of her head, she pulled the cart to the side.

'You're a damn fool, Ethan,' she whispered.

'I know.'

Ethan climbed from the cart. He was going to look in on Dale and Sarah in the back of the cart, but he didn't.

Sam jumped from his horse, shaking his head, and passed the reins to Ethan.

Ethan leapt into the saddle. He stared back at the cart as Sam joined Martha on the front. In a self-conscious gesture, he tipped his hat.

'You don't have to do this,' Martha whispered.

Ethan sighed, then swung round to face the trail back to Dirtwood.

'Trouble is,' he said, 'I never wanted to run.'

CHAPTER 13

Luke rode down Dirtwood's main road and reined in his horse beside the saloon. From inside, merry chatter emerged as Josh and his men embarked on their nightly attempt to drink the saloon dry.

With the light breeze whipping his coat behind him, Luke dismounted and stood a moment. He swung the reins around the rail and sauntered on to the board-walk. With his hat tipped back, he strode inside and glanced around the saloon.

Twelve people were there.

Josh glanced up from the bar and waved him closer.

'Who you looking for?' he asked.

Luke strode to the bar. 'Rock and Big Dawson ain't here.'

'I sent them to look for you.'

'Needn't have bothered. I'm back.'

Josh shrugged. 'Yeah. What you been doing? Started to think you weren't returning.'

'I just been around.'

Josh laughed. 'Our townsfolk ain't getting too uppity are they? You're all messed up.'

Luke rubbed his chin, feeling a bruise. 'Had to bang heads together to make myself understood.'

'When you want fun, bring us along to enjoy the show.'

'I know the score.' Luke rubbed another sore spot across his ribs. 'But this one was unscheduled.'

Josh poured a whiskey into a fresh glass and held it up to Luke.

'You ready for your drink yet? Or are you still anticipating it?'

'Still anticipating.' Luke glanced over his shoulder at the poker-game. 'Wouldn't mind joining in the fun here though.'

He grabbed a spare chair and wandered to the poker-table. To sit he swung his leg over the chair.

'Deal me in,' he said.

The dealer, Graham, grinned at the other poker-players, then dealt the next hand.

For the first five hands, Luke gained but then his mistakes piled up. Games of chance inside prison were common. But they usually involved betting on insects crawling up the walls, or on how many beetles were in the next meal. He knew enough about poker to follow what everyone did, but he didn't know enough to make headway.

When he received his first good hand, he bet heavily and everyone backed out. From the glances, everyone was marking him as even greener than before.

'I know how to make this more interesting,' Luke said, leaning back in his chair.

Everyone leaned forward.

'How?' Graham asked.

'We raise the stakes. I have two hundred dollars. That's my bet on the next hand.'

'We ain't interested.'

'Too big for you then?' Luke clattered his chair to the floor and leaned forward as if to rise. 'I'll have my drink instead.'

'No, wait,' Graham said, lifting a hand. 'We can match the stake.'

Luke rolled back into his chair. 'You sure? You just reckoned it was too big for you.'

Graham looked round the group.

Walt nodded. 'It is too high for any one of us, but we can raise that between us. I have twenty dollars.'

'Yeah, and I have thirty dollars,' Graham said, looking around the gathered men who pushed and shoved each other as they produced their part of the stake.

Within seconds, a pile of bills lay on the table.

Luke smiled and leaned forward. With his fingers whirling, he rummaged through the bills.

'Is everybody happy with the action they've staked?' he asked.

Graham looked round the group, then nodded.

'We are, but we're waiting to see your stake.'

Luke extracted his wad of bills and counted them on to the table.

'Just two people in the game,' he said, slipping the extra dollars back into his pocket. 'Me and your best player.'

'That'd be me,' Graham said to a chorus of agreement. 'What's your choice of game?'

'I ain't an expert on the names, but I'm used to a

simple kind. We deal two cards on the table. We both get five cards.'

Graham chuckled. 'This sounds like poker to me.'

Luke smiled. 'We change once. Then the best hand of five wins.'

As Graham received agreement to the bet from everyone, Josh strode to the table.

'Why you raising the stakes?' Josh asked.

Luke sighed. 'Because I am moving on and two hundred dollars is an odd amount to own. It ain't enough to live on but it doesn't make me poor. With four hundred dollars, I might be able to start a legitimate business. With nothing, I'll have to use my gun skills. So I'm prepared to risk leaving here with nothing against leaving here with four hundred dollars. This one hand will decide my future.'

Josh shrugged. 'A gamble in all ways.'

'Sure is.' Luke rocked forward in his chair and glanced around the table at Josh's grinning men. 'Are we ready to play poker?'

Everybody leaned forward as Graham dealt five cards to himself and Luke, turning over two cards on the table – the ace of hearts and the eight of clubs.

Luke pulled his cards along the table. He piled them on top of each other and slipped them close to his face. With his thumb and forefinger, he fanned open the cards, then closed them and placed them on the table.

He had three low hearts and two picture clubs.

'Dealer takes two,' Graham said, taking two cards from the pack.

Luke thought about trying for a flush. Then he smiled.

'Five.'

Everyone laughed, even Josh guffawing.

While biting his bottom lip, Graham dealt five new cards.

Luke lifted the cards to his face and fanned them out. He'd picked up two aces. He placed the cards face down on the table and pushed the bills into a neat pile beside the hold cards.

'If you want another five,' Graham said, chuckling, 'it'll cost you another two hundred dollars.'

'I'm fine with these. What you got?'

With deliberate slowness, Graham turned over each of his cards – two of hearts, seven of spades, queen of diamonds, eight of diamonds. He looked around the group, who muttered amongst each other. Then he spun over his last card – eight of hearts.

A huge explosion of sighing rippled around the group.

'With an eight in the hold, I'm claiming three eights,' Graham said, folding his arms and grinning. 'What you got?'

Luke lifted the edge of his cards and glanced at his two aces. He stared at the ace in the hold. He took a long breath. From the corner of his eye, he glanced at the half-filled whiskey glass on the bar.

He sighed. 'Nope. Beats me.'

'Yes,' Graham shouted and pounced on the pile of bills.

'Wait!' Luke roared. With his left hand, he lunged, catching Graham's hand before it reached the bills. He held it inches from the closest dollar bill. 'I ain't worked out what you've just done.'

'Game's simple,' Graham muttered. 'I have two eights. With the other eight in—'

'I know the result. I just ain't worked out how you got to it.'

Graham narrowed his eyes as everyone backed from the table.

'You accusing me of something?'

'Not just you. You ain't bright enough to cheat me on your own, but everyone had a stake, so you had help.'

Graham gulped and wrenched his hand away.

Luke pulled his gun. He blasted Walt through the chest and Davis deep in the guts. He swung the gun back to Graham before his scrambling hand had reached under the table for his own gun.

'You telling me who else helped you?' Luke roared.

'I was on my own,' Graham whispered, lifting his hands wide.

Luke shrugged and shot Graham through the forehead. Then he jumped up from the table and swung his gun in a steady arc around the circle of men.

'Anybody else want to admit they cheated me?'

One by one everybody shook their heads, most lifting their hands high from their gunbelts.

Luke finished his steady roaming of his gun with it aimed at Josh, who shook his head.

'You made a mistake, Luke,' Josh muttered. 'Graham wasn't cheating.'

'And?'

Josh stared hard at Luke. Then a smile appeared.

'Except Graham probably cheated every other time he played poker. Funny that you killed him the only time he wasn't.'

Luke let his stern gaze die and smiled too. 'And Walt and Davis?'

Farley joined Josh and shrugged. 'Who cares?'

Everybody laughed. To Josh's direction two men dragged the bodies back across the saloon.

Doc dashed from behind the bar and confirmed the three men were dead. Then they threw them through the back door.

Luke scratched his head. 'So you and me ain't got a problem?'

Josh shrugged. 'Nope. I didn't buy into that bet.'

Luke nodded and slipped his gun into its holster.

'Glad to hear it. I just shot three of your men and who knows, one day you and I might meet and I'd hate for us to be on the wrong side.'

Josh smiled. 'Men like Graham are in every saloon. I'll easily get more like him. You, though, are different. I don't want you as an enemy.'

'You're a wise man.' Luke smiled. 'Just like me.'

'You want that drink now?'

Luke smiled. 'Nope.'

Josh tipped back his hat and glanced outside.

'Why are you moving on? We have a good set-up here. I know you ain't enjoyed your revenge as much as you thought, but that ain't a reason to look elsewhere for something you won't find.'

'I reckon that things will change soon. I covered my tracks when I escaped, but the law ain't that stupid. They'll work out soon that I'm around these parts.'

Josh nodded at Luke's gun. 'Man with a fast hand like yours has nothing to fear.'

'Every man should feel fear if he's outnumbered. I'd

advise you to move on soon too, before they come looking for you.'

'They'll only be after you.'

'Perhaps, but somebody will decide that the infa-
mous outlaw Wiley Douglas is only a farmer and Sheriff
Ogden's death has no culprit. Or somebody will notice
that a bounty hunter is missing or that Cooper is late
with his deliveries. Then that somebody will decide
something is wrong in Dirtwood and come looking for
answers.'

Josh shrugged. 'Pity. I like it here. A man could get
used to drinking in this saloon.'

'I know. That's why I returned here tonight before I
left for good.'

Josh narrowed his eyes. 'But you ain't had that
drink.'

Luke shrugged. He strode to the table and collected
the scattered bills. He counted them into two piles and
pocketed one pile.

'See no reason to collect on that bet,' he said. 'We
have no way of knowing who really won.'

As everyone muttered approval, Luke pushed the
other pile of bills to the edge of the table.

'You're a right fair man,' one man said, reaching for
the bills.

Luke shrugged and turned over his cards. He shuffled the cards apart and stared at his two aces.

The nearest man followed his gaze, then looked at
Luke.

'What you playing at?' he muttered, his hand stray-
ing to his gunbelt.

Luke pulled his gun and shot this man through the

140

chest. He swung the gun round and blasted slugs into the nearest two men. Then he leapt to the floor and slid towards the bar. Scrambling on hands and feet, he dashed behind it as a volley of gunshots ripped into the side of the bar.

With his head down, Luke sidled to the middle of the bar and reloaded. He glanced at Doc who dashed back into his storeroom. Then he edged along the bar to the opposite end, always keeping his head down.

As he regained his breath, he counted through his successes. He'd walked into the saloon facing twelve men and he'd halved that number, but the remainder still contained Josh and Farley.

Timbers creaked as his opponents slipped behind cover.

'What're you trying to do?' Josh shouted from the saloon doors.

'Trying to leave here alive.'

'You have an odd way of going about it. We were no threat to you, Luke. You had my word.'

Luke cocked his head to one side, judging Josh's position. With his free hand, he wiped the sweat from his gun hand, then off his forehead.

'Yeah, but I've seen how you looked at me since Blake put ideas in your head. I have a price on my head. I'm everybody's fair game.'

Josh sighed. 'But not ours, Luke. If we tried to collect on you, we'd get ourselves killed.'

'You forget how I met Farley. He was telling a good tale in Hard Creek. He can charm his way into anybody's good books.'

Farley laughed. 'You're right, but we weren't turning you in.'

'I'd like to believe you.'

With low voices, Farley and Josh muttered to each other. Then a table scraped across the floor.

'You can,' Josh shouted. 'Come out. You'll get no retaliation.'

Luke grabbed a fallen glass. He knelt and pulled back his arm.

'I'll trust you. I'm coming out.'

He rolled the glass out from the bar.

Gunfire blasted around the glass, until Josh shouted for calm.

Luke laughed. 'Glad I tripped or you might have hit me.'

'Accident, Luke. We're edgy out here.'

Moving slowly, Luke slipped along the bar. A nearby timber creaked and he edged back under the bar as far as he could go.

A round of gunfire blasted, the shots smashing glass along the floor.

When the shots paused, Luke swung around the bar, taking the man who'd tried to outflank him through the neck. Then he swung back in.

'You still edgy out there?' Luke shouted.

Josh whispered low words. Farley replied.

Luke listened for further attempts to close on the bar but heard only their muted conversation.

'You have cover,' Josh shouted. 'But if needs be, we can wait all night and all day. You'll have to come out before too long.'

'And when I do, I suppose you'll be waiting?'

'Yeah. We didn't intend to take you before, but we do now. Being fast won't help you against five of us.'

'Ten minutes ago there were twelve of you.'

'That was before we knew what you were doing. We've trained our guns on the bar. The second you come out, you'll be full of lead.'

The swing-doors creaked. Then a screeching noise sounded from someone dragging another table across the floor. The back door creaked.

Luke nodded. They were getting into position. Someone was slipping outside to get into the store-room.

He flexed his hands, then swung up to slam his elbows on the bar. He fired at the nearest man, then leapt to the floor as gunshots peppered the bar.

He rolled over his shoulder and came up firing at another man who dashed at him. He ducked again, then rolled out from the bar, landing on one knee. He fired his gun empty of bullets, peppering his shots across everyone that he saw.

As men fell before him, he slipped back to lean against the bar. He didn't waste time on getting cover, reloading with a dexterity that didn't waste a second.

Even as he slipped in the last bullet, he pushed to his feet and faced the saloon. Gunsmoke was thick in the air, eddying over the bodies sprawled over tables and chairs.

In the confusion, Luke had lost track of how many he'd killed. He stood with his legs wide, alive to unexpected movements or sounds as he counted the bodies.

Seven bodies were in the saloon. With the three they'd thrown outside, that left two men alive. He glanced at the bodies again, confirming these missing men were Josh and Farley.

Luke glanced at the swing-doors just as he heard the cocking of a gun behind him. He half-swung then stopped and looked down.

'Guess that's you, Josh,' he muttered. 'You're the kind of man who hides when his men face danger.'

'I'm also the kind of man that survives,' Josh said. 'Put that gun back in its holster.'

Luke glanced at his gun hand and slipped the gun away. Josh pushed open the back exit and strode inside.

From outside, Farley wandered through the swing-doors and looked around the saloon, shaking his head.

'A year to get these people together,' he said, his voice high, 'and you've wiped them out in seconds.'

Luke shrugged. 'Yeah, but the way I see it, if we join forces, we don't need anyone else.'

Farley glanced at Josh.

'Ain't seeing it that way,' Josh muttered. 'If you'd suggested that ten minutes ago, I'd have joined you, but you've gone too far.'

Luke strode a long pace towards the centre of the saloon.

'Can't blame a man for asking.' Luke turned so that he faced the swing-doors, placing Farley before him and Josh behind him. He nodded to the gun in Farley's hand. 'Hope you're going to use that on me.'

Farley narrowed his eyes. 'What do you mean?'

'Your brother likes his bullwhip. I've lived my life with the gun. Don't want to die any other way.'

Josh chuckled. 'Dying from a gunshot in the back is no way for any man to die.'

144

'That doesn't worry me. After what I've done, I figured that I'd go that way and most people would see it as fitting.'

'In that case, I'm glad to oblige.'

Luke nodded. 'Just do one thing for me, Josh. When you shoot me, aim low. Lead in the guts finishes off any man, but a high shot often wings a man and he can take time to die.'

'And you deserve to go quick?' Josh muttered.

Luke shrugged and stared into Farley's eyes.

'What do you reckon, Farley?'

When Farley shrugged, Luke went for his gun. In an instant it came to hand and he ripped it out, blasting lead into Farley's guts before Farley had even reached his gun.

As Luke fired, he ducked, forcing his left shoulder down so hard he almost wrenched a muscle.

He swung round on his hip as a bullet ripped a furrow across his shoulder. As he fell, he fired before he'd even sighted Josh, taking his aim only from his hearing.

Even so, his shot blasted into Josh's side, Josh's gun flying from his grasp as Josh fired a second shot into the floor.

Lying on his side, Luke glanced at Farley, but his blood-coated body writhed on the floor, then stilled. He turned to Josh, who'd staggered back against the wall holding his chest.

'You should have listened to me,' Luke said, rolling to his feet. 'I told you to shoot low. If you'd listened, I wouldn't have avoided a bullet in the guts. Some people never like taking orders.'

'What you going to do?' Josh muttered, the pain narrowing his eyes.

Luke sauntered to the bar. After his earlier onslaught, just one bottle of whiskey had survived. He picked it up and rummaged through the broken glasses.

Doc slipped in from the back store. He joined in the search and found a whole glass. To Luke's nod, he poured a measure and held it out.

Luke took the glass. 'Thank you kindly.'

'Sure is great to get things back to normal,' Doc said. 'I didn't see what you did to Caleb Dalton but Felix and the rest had some answering to do. On behalf of the townsfolk, I'm obliged for what you've just done.'

'Obliged, are you? You served these men.'

Doc shrugged. 'I'm a businessman. I live with the times and tend my saloon. I don't take sides. I give drinks to whoever wants them.'

Luke sneered. 'That makes you the worst of all.'

He drew his gun and, with a flick of the wrist, shot Doc through the forehead.

As Doc slid to the floor, Luke poured a splash of whiskey from his glass on to the bar and turned to Josh.

'Why did you turn on us, Luke?' Josh whined. 'If you'd left, we wouldn't have come after you. We saw what you can do with that gun. We wouldn't take you on whatever the reward was.'

'Yeah. You ain't got enough sense to see the opportunity. Now, where is that bullwhip?'

'You wouldn't.'

The bullwhip lay against the wall. Luke smiled. He strode to the wall, grabbed the whip, and unfurled the

146

length. He ran his finger over the tip. Then he hurled it at the wall.

'You're right. I wouldn't do that. I may be like you, but then again, I ain't like you.' Luke turned and strode to the tangled pile of tables.

He gathered the strewn bills and lifted them to his pocket. Then sighing, he wandered to the bar and threw them on Doc's body.

'I'll say goodbye,' Luke said, tipping his hat to Josh.

'You ain't leaving me alive, are you? A man shouldn't have enemies.'

Luke shrugged. 'A man should always have enemies. It adds spice.'

'You'll regret those words one day.'

Luke swung the doors open and stood in the door-way, looking to the star-filled sky.

'One day,' he whispered.

CHAPTER 14

The farm was ahead, outlined against the night sky. But Ethan was only interested in the movement he'd seen.

Although the gesture didn't help, he lifted his hand to his brow and peered at his house. Again, something moved on the right-hand side.

Then somebody shouted. The words were indistinct but the tone was obvious. The person was searching Ethan's home and he was annoyed.

Ethan slipped from his horse and hefted his rifle – he was more comfortable with this familiar weapon. He tethered his horse to a tree and edged down the trail to his house. Fifty yards away, he saw the two horses at the side of his house and the open door.

'You sure?' someone shouted from near the horses. Ethan recognized Dawson's voice.

'Yeah. He's long gone,' Rock shouted from inside the house.

'Can't blame him. Luke has a history with this one.'

Dawson wandered around the house and paced to the door. He looked inside and wandered in.

With a final check that only two horses were outside,

Ethan dashed down the trail, covering as much distance as possible before the men emerged from his home. Ten yards from the doorway he hunkered down behind a bush and readied his rifle.

'He's left food,' Rock said, inside the house. 'You want some?'

'Nope. Let's check the other farms.'

'You go. I ain't had decent food since we came here.'

'I'll swing by on the way back.' Dawson appeared in the doorway and waved back inside.

Ethan firmed his gun hand and fired, taking him through the chest.

Dawson spun back and around. He clutched hold of the doorframe, then slid to the ground.

With his fingers shaking, Ethan reloaded and lifted his rifle.

'You're wrong,' Ethan shouted. 'We've decided to fight.'

Rock's hand edged around the doorframe. It touched the body lying in the doorway, then retreated inside.

'I'd spotted that,' he shouted.

'I'm giving you a choice. You can stay and fight, or you can return to Dirtwood and give Josh and Luke a message.'

'I'd like to hear that message.'

Ethan opened his mouth to shout his defiance. Then he realized that Rock's voice had come from the back of the house – there was a back door.

'Message is long,' Ethan shouted. 'You'd better come out so there can be no confusion.'

'I've taken messages to Josh before. I'll remember.'

Ethan smiled. Rock was even further back in the house.

149

He paced from his bush and slipped around the side of his house. He edged around the corner of the back wall. The back door was open. Worse, Rock's outline slipped around the opposite corner of the building.

Ethan edged to the back door. He slipped inside and through his home to the front door. Standing by the body, he glanced through the door, but outside the darkness was absolute, only the outlines of bushes and trees were visible against the night sky.

He cursed himself for losing sight of his quarry. Then he dashed to the back door, slipped outside, and followed Rock's route around the wall.

As he reached the corner, a gunshot blasted into the wall beside him and a second shot ripped his hat from his head. Ethan threw himself to the ground and peered in all directions, but he only saw the dark.

'You ready to give me that message?' Rock shouted.

Ethan cocked his head to one side, searching for the voice's location.

'I'm ready, if you're listening.'

'Go on. I'm sure I can give Josh your last words.'

Ethan rolled to his feet, then dashed back along the wall. Further gunshots blasted into the wall around him, but he reached the door at full tilt and leapt inside.

He dashed through the house to the body in the front doorway. He ripped Dawson's gun from its holster, then dashed outside to the bush he'd hidden in before.

There, he kept quiet.

'You'll come out soon,' Rock shouted from behind

the house. 'But if you don't, you can stay here until I fetch Josh.'

Ethan knelt and watched the horses. He put down the rifle and steadied his new gun over his arm, aiming at the side of his home.

Every few minutes, Rock taunted him with new offers to come out, but Ethan said nothing, keeping his only advantage – his unexpected location.

Two minutes later his persistence was rewarded when Rock slipped around the side of the house.

When Rock was half-way between the corner and the door, Ethan fired, aiming at his chest. The first shot missed and, with alarming speed, Rock turned and fired into the bush in which Ethan was hiding.

Ethan leapt from the bush, rolled over his shoulder and came up turned to Rock. He fired, again missing, Rock firing back, but on his third shot, Ethan hit him in the stomach.

Rock folded and landed on the ground, writhing.

Biting back his distaste, Ethan fired again at the body and it rose, fell, and then stayed still.

With a sickness in his gut, he pulled the bodies from his house and dragged them to the bushes. He freed the horses and trudged down the trail back to his own horse. He mounted it and headed to Dirtwood.

With his posture hunched, he spurred his horse to extra speed.

In a flurry of dust, he crested the last ridge before Dirtwood. He pulled back on the reins and had to bring his horse under control.

At the bottom of the hill, a rider approached and from the tall figure, Ethan recognized Luke.

With his horse set sideways, Ethan laid his rifle over his saddle. As Luke wasn't hurrying, he glanced at Dirtwood. No other riders approached.

When he was twenty yards away, Luke pulled to a halt.

'Howdy,' Luke shouted.

'Howdy to you.' Ethan nodded towards Dirtwood. 'I was sure you wouldn't have headed south. So now turn round and head back to town.'

'I ain't. My plans don't involve spending more time here.'

Ethan rubbed his chin. 'So you've had the drink you were anticipating?'

'Nope. I'm saving that for another day.'

'Did you tell Josh what we intend to do tomorrow?'

Luke smiled. 'Nope. But from what I heard, you've left. At least Josh was in town or he'd have noticed your quiet escape.'

Ethan frowned. 'Yeah. We're long gone and he'll never catch us. One day, we'll build a new Dirtwood some place even finer.'

Luke rubbed his forehead. 'From what I overheard at the barn, you ain't planning to build a new Dirtwood either. You intend to hide in the hills until it's safe to return.'

Ethan gritted his teeth. 'You overheard plenty.'

'I did and you're worth ten of every man in Dirtwood. And your new woman's worth five of every man too. You're the only ones who understand that you don't ignore or run from trouble. You face it head on and worry about the rest another day.'

'Ain't looking for understanding from you.'

'Never looked for it.'

'So why ain't you told Josh what we're doing?'

Luke glanced over his shoulder at the quiet town. He smiled.

'I could tell you a tale, but my reasoning is simple.'

'I know your reasoning and I ain't letting you leave thinking it's right. Martha said you noticed Dale.'

Luke nodded, his smile dying. 'I did.'

'Got news for you, Luke. He ain't yours.'

'You're making a big assumption.'

'He ain't!'

Luke lifted his hat and ruffled his hair. He replaced the hat and tipped it to the back of his head.

'Yeah, I know. You're his pa. You've looked after him and he always will be.'

'I'm his pa in every way.'

Luke glanced at Ethan's rifle and nodded.

'If you say so.' He sighed. 'Take my advice, Ethan. Stay out of Dirtwood tonight. You have the guts to face Josh and, if courage were enough, you'd beat him. It ain't. He'll kill you. Back up and defend the trail in case he comes after you, but don't look for that trouble.'

Ethan spat on the ground. 'These last few weeks I've heard that advice too often.'

'I'm sure you have, but this time it's coming from someone who knows what he's talking about. Josh doesn't know you've gone so you don't need to tell him. Every second until he finds out improves your chances.'

Ethan gripped his rifle tighter, then swung it down.

'If you ain't told him, guess that's good advice. But the second he leaves Dirtwood, he'll face me.'

Luke nodded. 'You're speaking sense and I wish you luck. But as an old friend, I have some more advice for you. You have a fine crop in the fields. Don't wait too long before you scout back to see what Josh is doing. I reckon he'll have other plans soon.'

'Do you know something I don't?'

Luke opened his mouth, then closed it. He shrugged.

'I know Josh's kind. I am one of his kind.' Luke glanced back at Dirtwood. 'In the few days I've been here, a whole mess of quarrels has built. Once your townsfolk ain't around to torment, it wouldn't surprise me if his men fell out over a poker-game. It just needs a wrong word and the lead will fly. Even Josh and Farley might face each other down.'

Ethan nodded. 'Hope you're right.'

'Reckon I will be.' Luke tipped his hat and pulled his horse around Ethan. 'I'll say goodbye.'

Ethan watched him pass. 'Where are you going?'

'That a-way,' Luke said, pointing ahead.

'Then keep going that a-way. I ain't lying to you. Soon as the law, or anyone else interested in you, passes through, I'll tell them where you went. Everyone in Dirtwood will celebrate when we hear they've found you and strung you up.'

'Never expected it any other way. I only ask you to do one thing for me.' Luke glanced sideways at Ethan. 'Look after Dale for me.'

As Luke trotted away, Ethan spat on the ground. Anger coursed through his body and he swung the rifle up. Without thinking, he blasted a slug into Luke's back.

Luke collapsed. To avoid sliding to the ground he grabbed his pommel.

Ethan ejected the spent cartridge and readied for

another shot, the rifle held high.

'Keep your hands on that pommel,' he muttered.

Luke righted himself and with a wide grimace, swung his horse round.

'You shot me in the back,' he said between gasps.

'Sure did. It's all your sort deserves. Now swing your horse around and head back to Dirtwood. I ain't making a habit of killing in cold blood. Doc Taylor can do some doctoring. He'll fix you up if you're quick.'

'What will Josh think when I arrive with a slug in me?'

'Don't care. I ain't taking your advice. I've had as much as I can take of people knowing what's best for me. Tell Josh what happened and tell him two more bodies are back at my farm with my bullets in them. Tell him I'm ready to take him on if he comes after us. I'm guarding every yard of the trail west. Any man that comes close will get what you got.'

Luke lifted his hand. He swayed to the side, then gripped the pommel to pull himself upright.

'I'll warn him.'

Ethan gestured with his rifle. 'There's more. After we've escaped, things will worsen for Josh. I'm on the outside and he's defending his patch. I can come when I want, pick his men off, and then leave. If he wants to live, he'd better scat. As for you, that's your warning, if you have any ideas about looking for me.'

'Yeah,' Luke gasped. 'I got it.'

With his shoulders hunched, Luke slipped his free hand through the reins and hurried his horse along three paces.

'And for the last time,' Ethan shouted. 'Dale ain't yours.'

With his teeth gritted, Luke glanced over his shoulder.

'I know. Dale couldn't be mine. I was just wondering.'

Ethan sighed. 'Stop wondering and get on back to Dirtwood.'

Ethan swung his horse to the side. He kept his rifle trained on Luke until Luke's steady pace had moved him out of range. Then he galloped away. At the next ridge, he glanced back.

In the distance, Luke's swaying form approached Dirtwood.

Ethan sneered. He swung his horse around and headed west, his rifle loaded and ready to face any trouble.

CHAPTER 15

Hunched in the saddle, Luke rode back into Dirtwood. Without directions, his horse aimed for the saloon and halted.

Luke released his tight grip on the reins. He rolled from the saddle and landed in a heap on the ground. He lay regaining his breath, then pushed to his feet. With his body doubled over he staggered on to the boardwalk and gripped the saloon's doorframe.

From the corner of his eye, he glanced at the darkened fields beyond the edge of town. Dawn glowed on the eastern horizon, but Ethan had gone. With a nod and a smile west, he levered his body as straight as possible and stumbled inside the saloon.

Josh was slumped over the bar, a bottle of whiskey before him and his gun lying propped against a whiskey-glass. As Luke staggered another step, Josh looked up, his eyes unfocused. Around his feet, a pool of blood had spread.

Luke gripped the doorframe, knowing that if he let go he'd fall to the floor.

'Morning, Josh,' he whispered.

Josh nodded. 'Guessed you wouldn't want to go

through life with me as an enemy.'

Luke forced himself to release the doorframe. As he expected, he swayed forward and he thrust out a leg to stop himself falling on his face. He tipped his hat, suppressing a wince.

'You guessed right. Don't want a lifetime of looking over my shoulder.'

Josh nodded and edged his hand to his gun. His fingers shook as he slotted in five bullets. Then he grabbed the whiskey-bottle and poured whiskey over the glasses on the bar. He picked a glass that had received a fair measure and pushed it along the bar.

Luke took a deep breath and staggered to the bar. He slumped against it and grabbed the glass.

Josh knocked back his drink and stared at the trail of blood leading to the door.

'You've been hit,' he said with a forced smile.

Luke returned the grim smile. 'I'd spotted that.'

'What happened?'

Luke gulped back a twinge of pain that coursed through his guts.

'You is what happened.'

Josh shrugged. 'I didn't hit you.'

'Somebody did. In the heat of fighting I shrugged it off, but it opened up when I rode out of here and I'm bleeding like a stuck pig.'

Josh chuckled. 'Glad to hear it. Take that drink and I can finish the job.'

Luke placed his glass on the bar. With one hand, he pushed from the bar and stood hunched.

'I've anticipated this drink for seven years. I can wait a while longer.'

Josh swung round. His foot slipped in the pool of blood at his feet and he had to right himself. Moving slowly, he straightened and swayed back and forth.

'That's a mistake. Take your drink before I kill you.'

Luke shook his head and took another pace from the bar.

'Maybe later.'

Josh grimaced and smoothed his jacket, running his hand through the thick blood. He glanced at his hand and wiped it on a rare clean spot on his trousers.

'Even with a bullet in you, I guess you're fast, so I'll go first.'

Luke nodded. He took a deep breath, the movement sending a sharp jolt of pain writhing through his guts. He winced.

Josh whirled his arm to his holster.

For the first time in his life, Luke put effort into grabbing his gun. He swung the gun up, aiming it at Josh.

With his gun arm raised, Josh glared at him.

'What you waiting for?' Luke muttered.

'You ain't fired either,' Josh said, nodding towards Luke's gun.

'I asked first.'

Josh staggered a pace. With a leg thrust forward, he stopped himself falling. He straightened and held his gun arm across his chest.

'I've spent the last few minutes realizing I ain't got the guts to kill myself. You can do it for me.'

Luke smiled. He placed the cool barrel of his gun against his forehead, then aimed it back at Josh.

'I'd figured that you ain't got the guts to die too. I want you to live long enough to tell everybody how I saved Dirtwood just because . . .' Luke winced, the room darkening as he stared at Josh. 'The reason doesn't matter. But I'd like everyone to know I died a hero after all the wrong I did here.'

Josh snorted. 'Your type don't get to be heroes.'

'Guess you're right.'

With a whirl of his arm, Luke fired, putting a bullet through Josh's guts and a second through his chest a moment later.

Josh spun round, blood splattering as he collapsed in a lifeless heap.

Luke underhanded his gun on to the bar and staggered a pace. To stop himself falling he grabbed the bar.

With a hand that shook for the first time in his life, he grabbed his glass of whiskey. He slipped, both elbows landing on the bar, the whiskey sloshing over his hands. The acrid smell filled his lungs, washing away the smell of gunpowder and blood.

With his guts burning, he angled the glass to pour some whiskey away. Then without pouring, he set the glass down and stared at the whiskey.

In his weakened state his elbow slipped and his head slumped to rest on his arm. With his head lying sideways, Luke sighed and licked his lips.

It was dark beyond the end of the bar.

'Anticipating you kept me alive for the last seven years,' he whispered. 'Let's see how long you can keep me alive now.'